I'M NOT SCARED OF YOU OR ANYTHING

Stories by
JON PAUL FIORENTINO

Illustrations by
MARYANNA HARDY

I'M NOT SCARED OF YOU OR ANYTHING

Stories by
JON PAUL FIORENTINO

Illustrations by
MARYANNA HARDY

anvil
PRESS

*Chris
most of the fucking stories are legit*
short stories
xoxo Jon

Copyright © 2014 by Jon Paul Fiorentino
All rights reserved. No part of this book may be reproduced by any means without the prior written permission of the publisher, with the exception of brief passages in reviews. Any request for photocopying or other reprographic copying of any part of this book must be directed in writing to access: The Canadian Copyright Licensing Agency, One Yonge Street, Suite 800, Toronto, Ontario, Canada, M5E 1E5.

Anvil Press Publishers Inc.
P.O. Box 3008, Main Post Office
Vancouver, B.C. V6B 3X5 Canada
www.anvilpress.com

Library and Archives Canada Cataloguing in Publication

Fiorentino, Jon Paul, author

    I'm not scared of you or anything / Jon Paul Fiorentino; Maryanna Hardy, illustrator.

Short stories.

ISBN 978-1-927380-94-9 (pbk.)

    I. Hardy, Maryanna, 1977-, illustrator II. Title.

PS8561.I585I4 2014   C813'.6   C2014-900725-6

Editor for the press: Brian Kaufman
Art: Maryanna Hardy
Design: Jon Paul Fiorentino
This book is set in Caslon and Museo Slab

Represented in Canada by the Publishers Group Canada
Distributed by Raincoast Books

The publisher gratefully acknowledges the financial assistance of the Canada Council for the Arts, the Canada Book Fund, and the Province of British Columbia through the B.C. Arts Council and the Book Publishing Tax Credit.

Printed and bound in Canada

I never told a joke in my life.
—Andy Kaufman

CONTENTS

I'M NOT SCARED OF YOU OR ANYTHING	9
PILLOW FIGHT	21
IT SEEMS LIKE SEX IS A WEIRD THING THAT USED TO HAPPEN TO ME SOMETIMES	29
#SWEETPROTIPS	45
CRITICAL THEORY ARCHIE	51
LIFE IS DIFFICULT BUSINESS, PERRY	59
THE PARABLE OF BRYAN DONG	75
INVIGILATOR	87
THE PROBLEM WITH LESLIE	103
PEN PALS	111
SYSTEMA VLAD	125
WHEN IT GOT A LITTLE COLD	147
TEEN WOLF QUOTES SLAVOJ ŽIŽEK	155
MR. SPOCK SAYS THINGS FROM EPISODES OF *GIRLS*	161
JON PAUL FIORENTINO INTERVIEWS HIS MOTHER	167

I'M NOT SCARED OF YOU OR ANYTHING

Here's what happened, Ingrid. I was shocked to see you. The bar you walked into is undoubtedly *my bar*. I live across the street for Christ's sake. They have a special tall glass just for me for my double vodka sodas. You know all this. If you don't want me in your life then perhaps you should not go to the bar where I always am. Anyways, I was pretty nerve-wracked to see your weird face, Ingrid. It was only the second time I have seen your weird face since you returned from your work assignment in the United Arab Emirates, and it has been hard for me to come to terms with the fact that you are here, but you are not here with me. You should know by now that this is all I want.

I was glad to hear about your cousin Maria's successful liver transplant and I was truly enjoying our conversation, Ingrid. I was happy we could sit down, on that patio, at *my bar*, and communicate the way people might in the real world. But here's what happened. And I hope it makes you understand a little bit better about that night.

Around two hours before I headed to *my bar*, I had ordered pot from my pot delivery guy. I don't know if you recall from our eight-month relationship, but I really like to smoke the pot on the regular in order to forget all of those awful things that happened to me and continue to happen to me. Anyways, it was taking, like, forever, so I cancelled the delivery. I had to get downtown by 11 pm to meet friends and I can't properly go downtown to meet friends without having a double vodka soda in *my glass* at *my bar* first. As you were telling me about Maria and your family's struggles to find the right donor, I noticed my pot delivery guy bounding up my stairs. He was actually bounding. I wish you could have seen it.

I suppose if I weren't so panicky, I could have said, "Hey, Ingrid, check out the guy bounding up my stairs!" But I did not do that and there is no going back. So when I dropped my cigarette and ditched my drink and sprinted across the street, that's why. It was the pot guy. I'm not scared of you or anything.

So I don't know how much of the rest you saw, so I will just tell you. I bought three ounces of "White Widow" from Jeremy, the pot guy. And then he bounded down the stairs and I sauntered down shortly after. I was about to

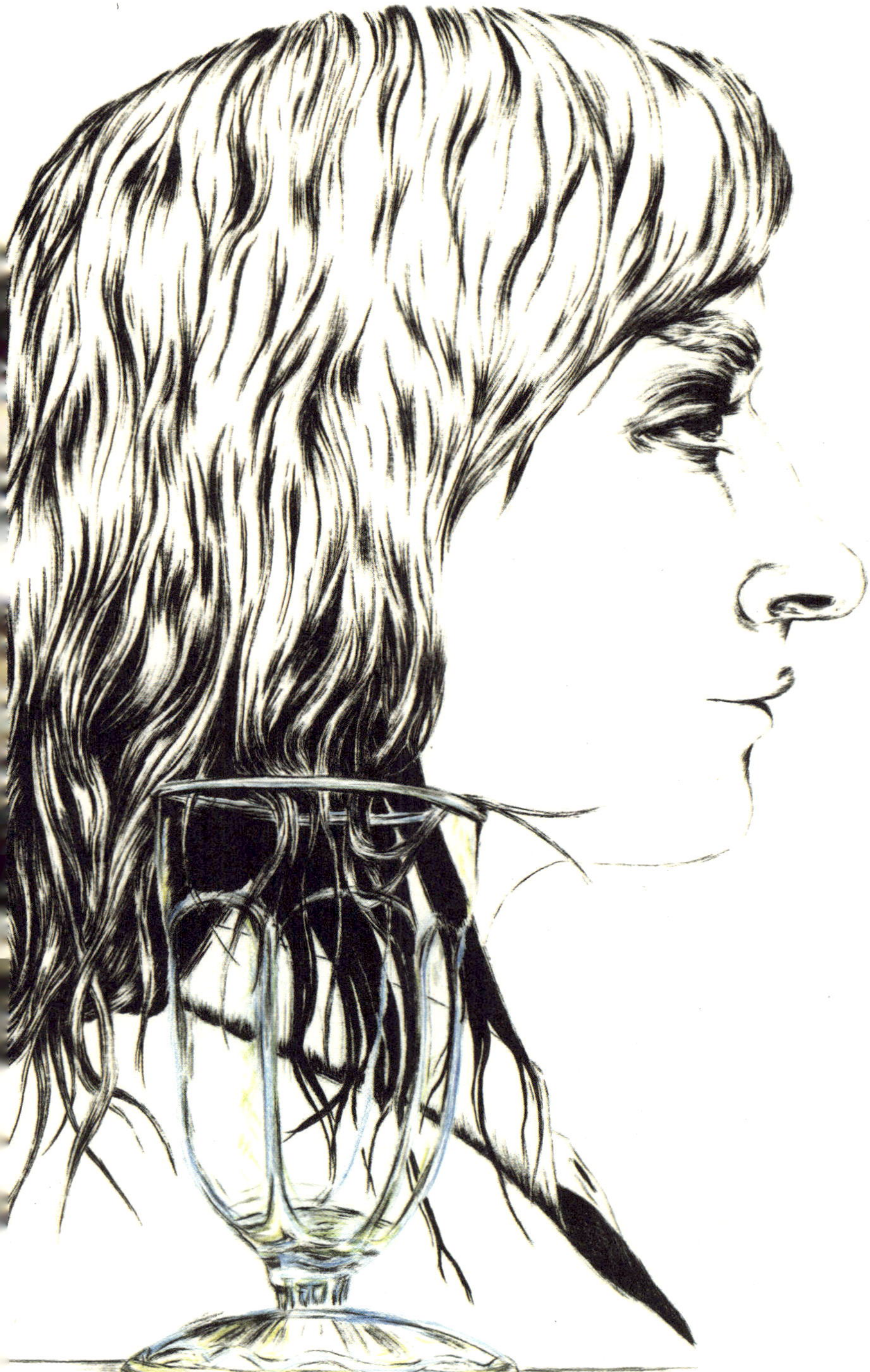

rejoin you across the street when suddenly, as things often happen in stories, a blinding light shone right in my face. I squinted and quickly realized that it was a police searchlight. I froze just like a guy in a police searchlight, which, indeed I was. I couldn't see beyond the cruiser car. I don't know if you were looking. It seems to me that you probably were on account of the brightness of the searchlight. Ingrid, I honestly did not know what to do. It occurred to me that the police would likely stop me if I jaywalked. I glared directly at the officer in the driver's seat and declared, "I am not going to jaywalk!" Did you hear this? I said it really loud. I stepped back onto the sidewalk and gingerly made my way to the corner where I could cross in a legal and gingerly fashion. The searchlight followed me. As I crossed the street, legally, at the next green light, the police car did a u-turn (an illegal one I might add) and kept its light on me. I felt like I was on stage, walking toward you, Ingrid. I was exceptionally nervous but there was this strange and beautiful sense of theatre that I thought you might appreciate if you were watching, which again, I assumed you were. But when I arrived on the patio, you were gone. I don't know when you bailed, but it was crushing to think that you missed this spectacle. Do you miss me?

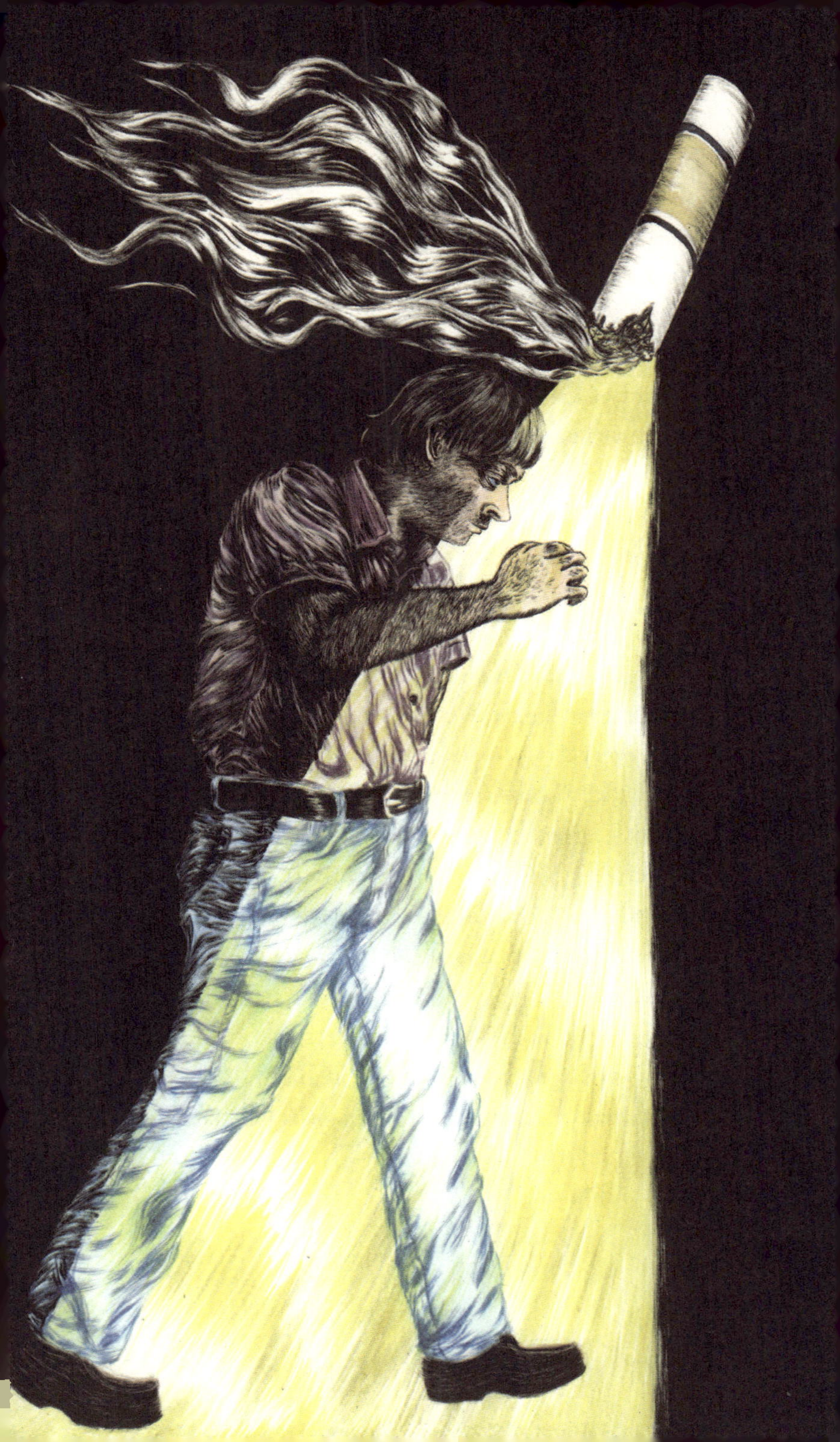

More things happened, Ingrid. It would be irresponsible not to tell you of these things. I left *my bar* and I walked toward downtown. The police were still there. But the searchlight was off. They slowly trailed me for a block or two until I hailed a cab. And that was that.

I met Jason and Clara downtown at that bar we used to have veggie burgers at. You know the one. *Our bar?* I suppose I was a little shaken from the police thing. But if I'm being honest, which I am, I was more shaken by seeing you and your weird face. Because I still love you and your weird face so much.

Ingrid, I don't know exactly how to say this because it will sound strange. But the rest of the night had pretty much everything to do with the dude from Iron Maiden. I don't really know the band, and I don't think you do either. But I want to say that he was the bassist from Iron Maiden, but I am not entirely sure if that's the case. The bartender pointed him out as "the dude from Iron Maiden," and so that is what I will refer to him as. He was alone but looking for company. He asked Clara and Jason and me if we knew what a Baby Aspirin was. I assumed he was not referring to an actual Baby Aspirin (which would clearly be some sort of Aspirin for babies) but, in fact, some sort of alcoholic shot. So I said no. And so did Clara and Jason.

"It's vodka, orange juice, and Triple Sec!" he said. "It's fuckin' delicious!"

He ordered a round for the four of us as we all took seats up at the bar. The Baby Aspirins, I have to admit, were pretty fuckin' delicious. Clara and Jason started making out and their hands got real busy on each other. The dude from Iron Maiden said, "Right on." And his hands got a little busy on Clara and Jason.

I'm not going to lie to you, Ingrid, the dude from Iron Maiden seemed magical. He was like an old mystical dude who just lifted everyone's spirits. I have never really understood the appeal of any kind of music that wasn't adult contemporary. But I have to admit that his presence alone made me want to buy an Iron Maiden t-shirt at the very least. But I was still sullen. Sullen because of the events that took place earlier in the night regarding you and your weird face and the police and the searchlight.

The dude from Iron Maiden looked me square in the eyes and said, "Do you know what your problem is, bub?" I had to say no. Although I am aware of all of the problems I currently have. I just didn't know which one was the one he meant. "Well neither do I. Because I don't fuckin' know you. But if I were to guess, I would say it's that you are a massive pussy." Then he slapped me on the back and said, "Live a little!" and ordered another round of Baby Aspirins.

The Baby Aspirins were pretty fuckin' delicious again. He yanked my barstool closer and gave me a stern-yet-tender look. "Listen, bub. I'll level with you. You know about Iron Maiden, right? You know why we are the number one band in the world?" Again, I had to say no. "Magic, bub. We're all card-carrying wizards. Real-life fuckin' wizards."

"Really?"

"Black magic is the key to our success. I am the senior wizard. I can cast any spell and it instantly will become reality."

"Gosh."

"Seriously, bub. If you tell me the thing you want most in this world, I will make it happen."

Ingrid, I have to tell you the truth. I asked him to make you love me like you used to and for us to be together. The dude from Iron Maiden laughed a deep, echoing belly-laugh, interrupting Jason and Clara's grope session and getting the attention of the entire bar. "I'm no wizard, you idiot! I'm just fuckin' with you, you fuckin' fuckwit." Everyone laughed at me. But honestly, Ingrid, how was I to know? He seemed like a magical wizard in pretty much every way. Then the dude from Iron Maiden draped his arms around me like a mother condor. "Listen, kid: there are a million things in this universe you can have and there are a million things you can't have. It's no fun facing that, but that's the way things are."

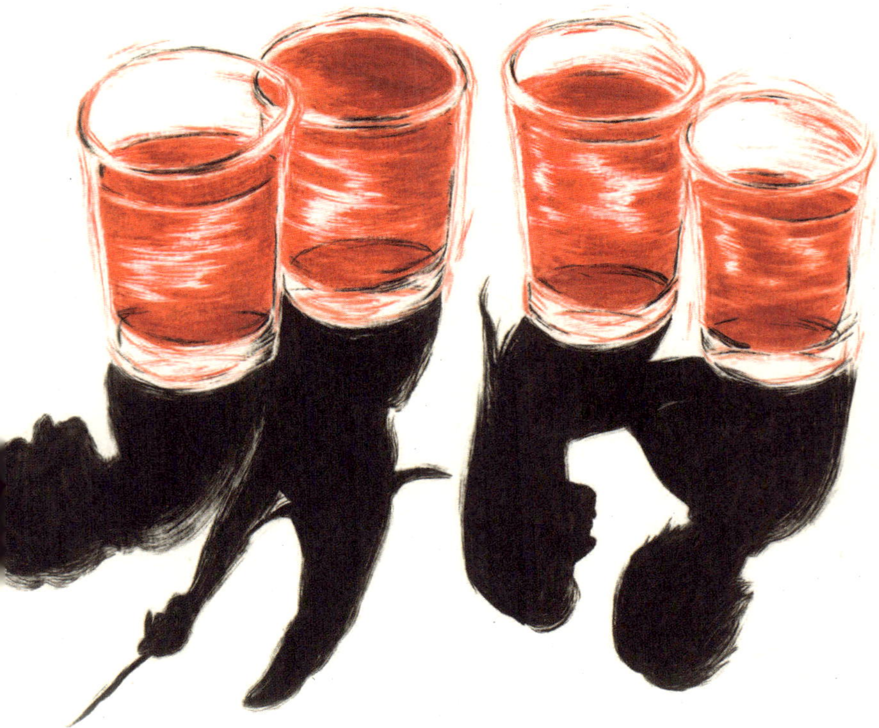

Ingrid, you know that I have a problem with confrontation, but I could not let this stand. "You stole that from Captain Kirk! That's what Captain Kirk says to Charlie X in the episode, 'Charlie X'!"

"That is true. But it doesn't make what I said any less true. Hey, fuckers, let's hit the strip club! Strippers and booze on me!" Jason and Clara were ecstatic. I remained hunched over. Still. Sullen.

"You guys go ahead. I have some big-time thinking to do," I said.

And so they went. Jason and Clara and the dude from Iron Maiden. Off into the steamy Montreal night. Off to enjoy strippers and booze the way well-adjusted, happy people would do in such a context. I realize what you might be thinking, Ingrid. I should have gone with them. If only for the life experience or the story. I will not get another chance to spend quality time with the dude from Iron Maiden. I realize this. But I want you to realize something too: I said no to the dude from Iron Maiden. And I said no to strippers. I will always be loyal to you.

PILLOW FIGHT

I first discovered I had a gift for pillow fighting when I was a young boy of eight and my dead older sister, Marjorie, who wasn't dead at the time, was having one of her regular pre-teen sleepovers. Marjorie enjoyed punching me, but Marjorie's friends enjoyed practicing kissing with me in order to prepare for their inevitable dating lives. I, even at the age of eight, was an object of desire. Gladys, Marjorie's best friend, initiated a pillow fight with me. They stood on Marjorie's bed and swung away at each other, giggling and generally enjoying the moment. Then I belted her so hard on the head with my double-soft feather pillow that she fell over and fractured her skull on the night table. Gladys turned to a life of drugs and home invasions in her twenties and I felt partially responsible for her downward life trajectory. And then when Marjorie's life fell apart and she joined her best friend in a life of petty crime and illicit drugs, I suppose I blamed Gladys for enabling her. Anyway, it was then and there, in my sister's bedroom, that I truly knew the power of my stroke. I swore I would only pillow fight again under conditions that were safe and guaranteed by a legitimate sanctioning body.

Every competitive pillow fight league in the city was designated as women-only. I had to lobby the Montreal Recreation Board for a full calendar year before they let me compete. My bureaucratic victory was consummated by the invocation of the rules and regulations of the Montreal Recreation Board, specifically, Sub-section 7.6, Item 7.601, which states: "Participation in any intramural sport shall not be denied to anyone on the basis of race, colour, religion, national origin, gender, age, disability, citizenship, veteran status, or sexual orientation." Had the board not been so sloppy in the authorship of their rules and regulations, I may not have had the opportunity to compete at the highest possible level of pillow fighting. Now five games in, my pillow fight record was two and three. I was under .500, but I was also a rookie. And the women I was fighting were seasoned veterans of the pillow fight circuit. One of my victories was accomplished by surrender on the part of my opponent. The other was won by pin-hold. My losses were all the result of the judges' decision, which led me to believe that there was a bias against me in the community. Organized sport is often rife with dirty politics.

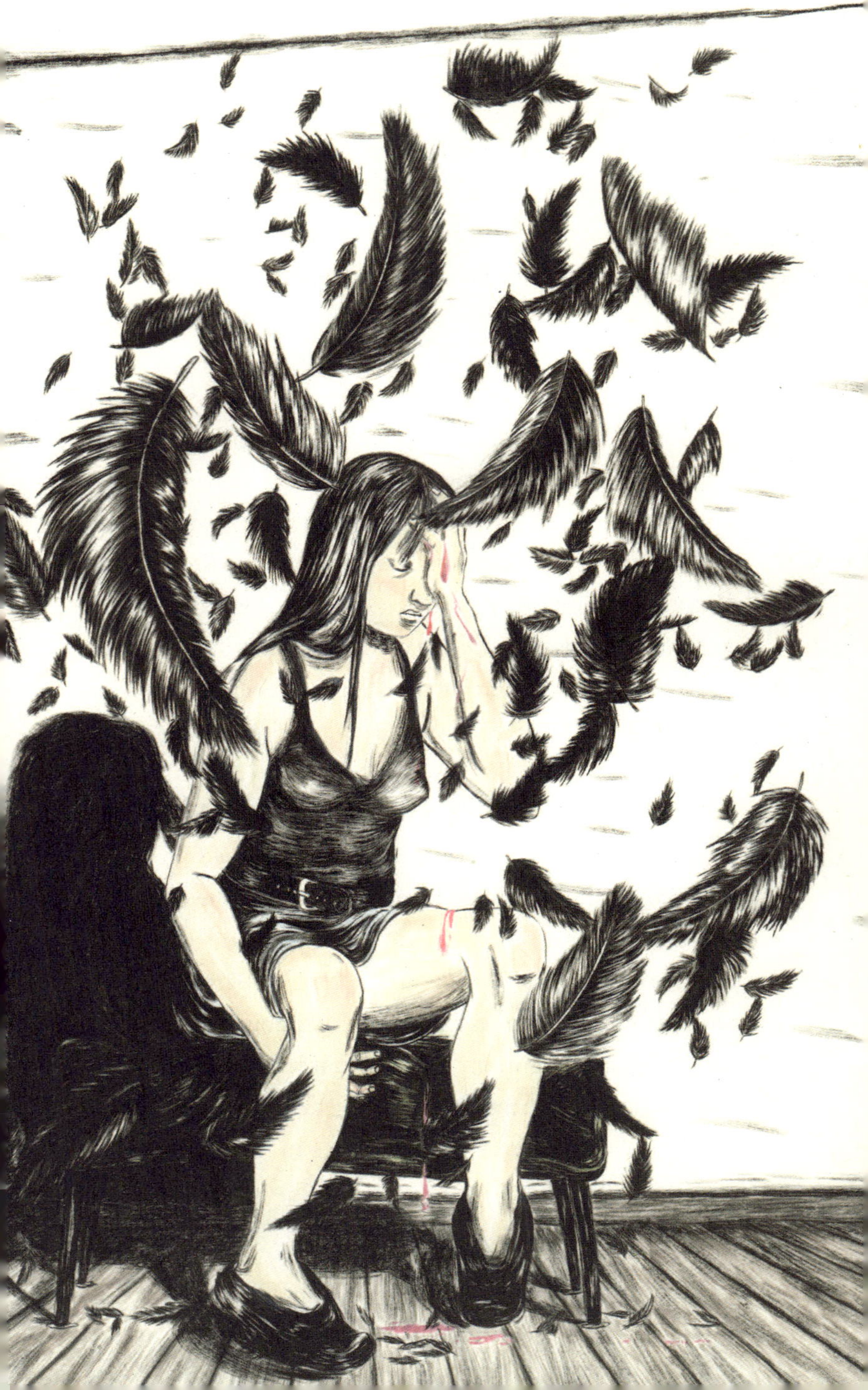

The specific circuit I had chosen to participate in is called the Montreal Central Pillow Fight League. I had chosen this specific league because, unlike the other Pillow Fight Leagues in the city, this one held its matches not in a dive bar but in a fairly respectable establishment called Café Arts/Maison du Coffee et Bière. There were fewer local boozehounds to heckle me as I honed my craft. I needed to block all distractions from my mind, to forget about the stigma of being the only male, the condescending and downright cruel attitude of my pillow fight peers, and the consistent rumours that the Montreal Recreational Board had already begun the process of redrafting their rules and regulations. None of this mattered when it was time to enter the ring, clutch my lucky Queen size K-Mart brand aromatherapy pillow, and start swinging.

The Montreal Central Pillow Fight League Champion, Constance Cummings, had defeated me already this year and was, without a doubt, the queen bee of the Montreal pillow fighting community. I had always dreamed of being the queen bee, but I had a hard time preparing for this match. Marjorie was gone, and her absence was the only ever-present thing in my life. I put on my lycra, one-piece, lime green uniform with matching headband and set off for the café. I preferred not to change in the washroom at the café for fear of fungal infections such as ringworm or *Tinea pedis*. Public washrooms were never my cup of tea, as it were.

The pillow fight match began slowly with Cummings and I sparring with each other at half-speed, and using footwork to establish both territory and rhythm. Cummings began to dominate the match in the second round. I did not block her heavy blows effectively and I began to feel defeated. My mind could not free itself from thoughts of Marjorie, her suspension from nursing school, her brief career as a cat burglar, the botched home invasion, the shotgun wound, the resulting death.

In the midst of the pummeling I was taking I felt a surge of energy. I experienced many things at once. Anger. Rage. Confusion. Hunger. Itchiness. Something entered me. Not literally. Some sort of non-literal thing. There was a beast inside me. Again, not literally. A figurative beast. I took a step back and glared at Cummings, and all I could see was Gladys. I was transported back to that fateful night when I had first discovered my talent. I started landing two-hander after two-hander to Cummings's face, fury and feathers flying. I pirouetted and executed an attack of equal grace and ferocity. I pinned her. It felt good to win. I looked down toward hell and said, "This one's for you, Marjorie!" I wonder if she heard me.

IT SEEMS LIKE SEX IS A
WEIRD THING THAT USED TO
HAPPEN TO ME SOMETIMES

The truth is I was a very disturbed individual. I still am. But I am at peace with it now. Not too long after I began to experience all of the panic attacks and all of the sadness attacks, I signed up for a screening interview to ascertain whether or not I was a suitable candidate for cognitive therapy.

My sadness was profound and it struck me at particular times. It had little to do with the weather or whether I was alone, which of course, I was. In fact, the sadness was acutely linked to the observation of other people's happiness. For instance, if I were on the bus and I were to see two people laughing or enjoying each other's company in any way, it would strike — as if all of the heartbreak and depression and anxiety that ever existed was heaped upon my shoulders and, more accurately, my brain. I would imagine enjoying such moments with someone who surely does not exist and never will. The thing about the sadness was that it was too unpredictable, and yet way too predictably abject to bear. The task at hand was to distract myself, to immerse myself in new life experiences. I had to move away from a life of introspection and self-torture and move toward a life of many interests, of even more experiences. But I would need help. I was only one man. Still am.

The flyer on the bulletin board said: "Are you depressed? Are you tired of taking anti-depressants? Do you want to take your own life? Are you ready to take your own life back in your hands instead of just taking it? If you've answered yes to at least two of these four questions, then you may be a suitable candidate for cognitive therapy!" I thought about it and my answers were yes, no, no and yes. Since I had answered yes to two or more of these questions, I decided I should really call the number of the Twin Spirits Homeopathic Cognitive Therapy Centre for Wellness. The receptionist said I was lucky — it turned out they had an open appointment the very next day!

As I strolled home that night, I looked up at the stars; the sky seemed to have been covered with some sort of epiphanic spackling. The cool Montreal air was soothing and the evening sky reminded me of my bedroom when I was a child. I'd had glow-in-the-dark star stickers all over my bedroom ceiling and when my mother would turn out the light, I would stare at the astronomically correct star field until all of the worries, embarrassments, and bruises of the day seemed inconsequential. Or less consequential. I guess I'm trying to say that the night sky was soothing that night. I got home, slid into my Buck Rogers pajamas and tucked myself in after a brief Google interlude in which I discovered some of the tenets of cognitive therapy. My eyes closed as I dopily began to formulate my responses to the questions I was anticipating.

It turned out that the Twin Spirits Homeopathic Cognitive Therapy Centre for Wellness was located in the Royal Victoria Hospital's psych ward. It was a pristine and promising environment. I headed toward the nurses' station and announced my arrival. A perky bee-hived nurse in a teal uniform greeted me with what seemed like a forced smile and gestured for me to sit down and so I did. A striking teenage girl with glassy eyes shuffled by in a hospital gown and smiled at me. I couldn't help but feel a sense of peculiar sadness. I wondered what mental affliction she had. I wanted to ask but that seemed inelegant. Another patient, an older gentleman with long, wispy gray hair, shuffled by. He sipped on a Diet Orange Crush through eight straws that had been crammed into the opening of his can. He offered me a sip and I declined.

After about half an hour, two thirty-something bearded men, one with a blue argyle sweater vest, and the other with a light brown tweed blazer, approached me.

"Mr. Marr?" The man with the sweater vest asked.

"Yes."

"I'm Dr. Galloway and this is my associate, Dr. Scholl."

"Hello!" I said, in a tone entirely too enthusiastic. I guess I was nervous!

"Please. Come with us."

The room was completely unfurnished and completely white. There were three chairs. Two were quite nice: expensive rolling and swiveling office chairs that looked like they provided more than adequate lumbar support. The third was a simple old wooden chair. I was ushered to the wooden chair, facing my two inquisitors. I thought it would have been a nice gesture, as I was technically the guest, for them to offer me one of the comfier chairs. But alas.

The questions began:

"Please answer with a 'true' or 'false' to the following statements, Mr. Marr," Sweater Vest said. "Number one. Others make me angry."

"They most certainly do! But only grown-ups and cruel people. I have nothing against the kind-hearted, chil-

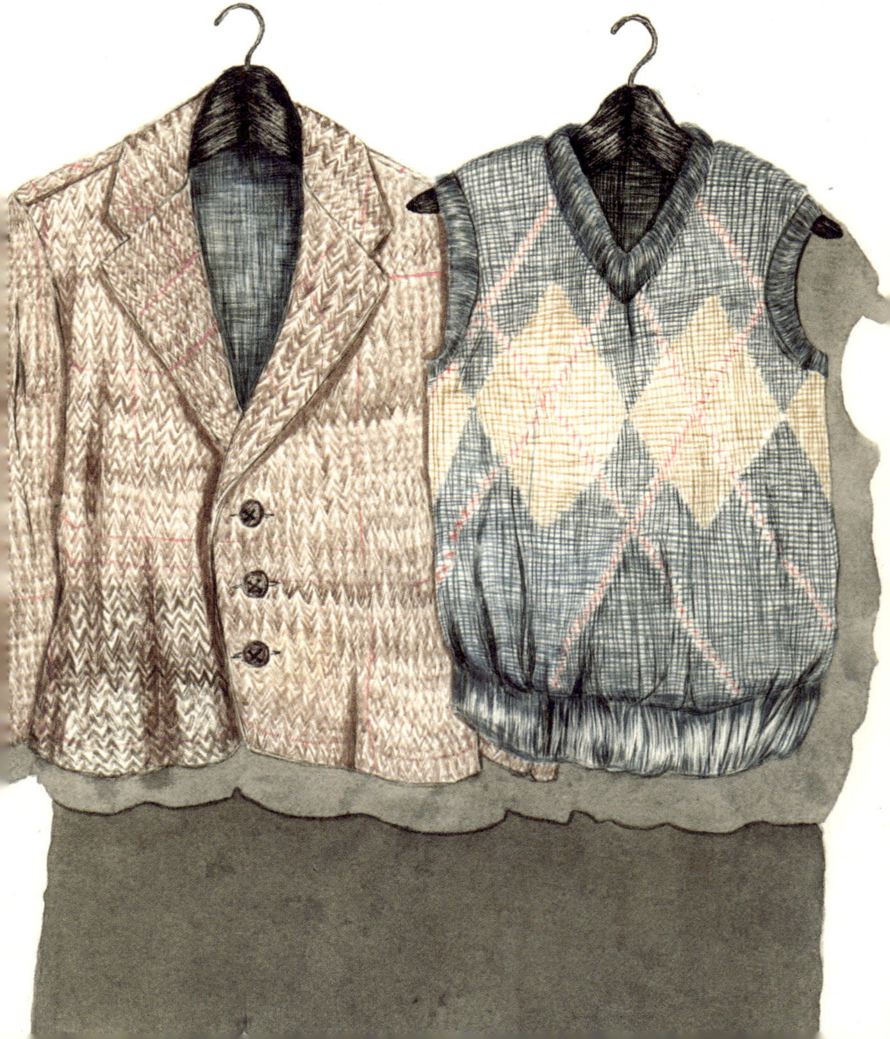

dren or the child-like. They are the inheritors of the Earth! I think that's in the Book of Mormon."

"Number two. At times I worry about..."

"This is not a true or false question is it? If it is, I suppose I would have to say true. I worry about sharks. I know it's irrational, being so far away from sharks, as I am in the middle of the city. But definitely sharks. Real sharks and also animatronic talking sharks. Also, I don't want to be seen as needy. In fact I would say I *need* to appear that I'm not needy."

"Mr. Marr, You didn't let me finish the question."

"Oh, I am sorry. I do tend to ramble when I get nervous or aroused."

"OK. Number two, again. At times I worry about my mortality."

"False. Because there is no God. And if there were a God, he would be mortal too, like that guy in the Bible, Moses?"

"Right. OK. Number three. I tend to ruminate about the past."

"False. Although I must add that I regret never having lived with anyone other than myself. But, recently, it occurred to me that I prefer to live alone. I'm not saying that because I'm alone. I have just acquired a particular contentment with the company of my own thoughts, as

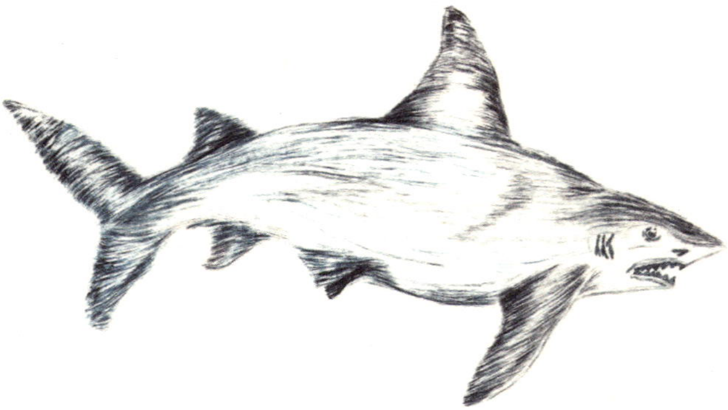

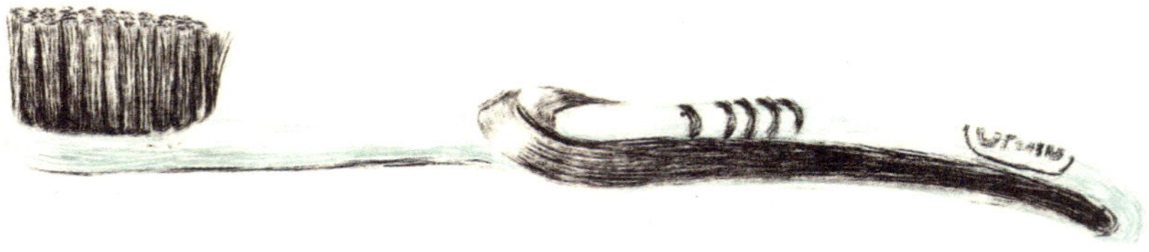

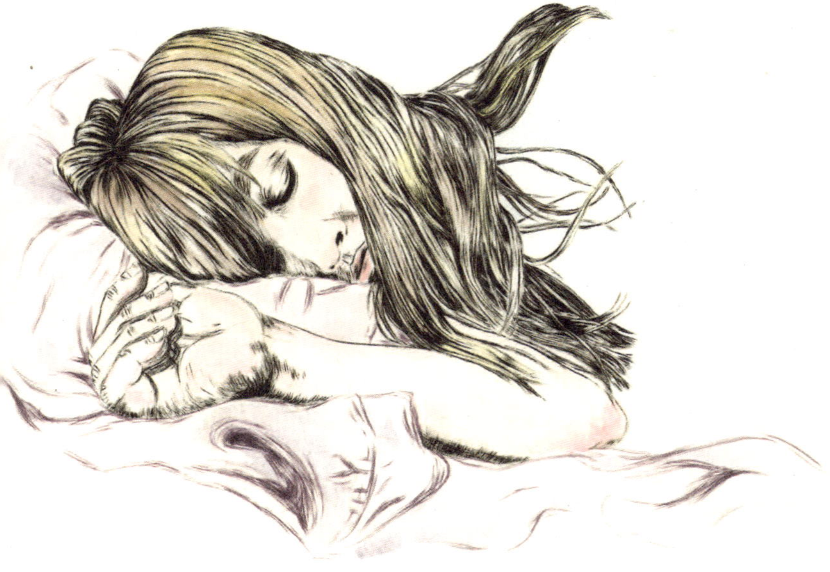

demented and disturbing as they may be. Also, I'm not sure if what I just said about my preference and contentment is true."

"Number four. Nasty names naturally hurt people."

"False. Except for words like fucking asshole and fucking fuckface and fucking cunt and so forth. Those words can sting."

"Number five. Most impulses should be squelched."

"True. However, I just had the strangest desire to get my hair cut in a Wal-Mart and so you know what I did? I went and got a haircut in a Wal-Mart. No joke. Can you imagine? I wish my mom were alive to see that shit go down! But I guess, in the end, I don't know what the real point of giving into one's impulses is. It turns out that life is a swirling vortex of despair. But the new IKEA catalog looks promising!"

"Number six. I have some flaws right now that I could stand to fix."

"True. But you know what? When I look in the mirror, that is to say, when I look at myself in the mirror, I think to myself: well done, Steven. I am thirty-six years old. I'm diabetic, asthmatic, photosensitive, and wickedly depressed, but I have most of my hair and I have avoided hard drugs for the most part. Oh and by the way, diabetes is just one of an astonishing number of things I have in common with Howard Hughes!"

"Number seven. It is healthy to revisit your youth on a frequent basis."

"False. Although I was watching the movie *Teen Wolf* recently and it occurred to me, and stay with me here: *Teen Wolf* is actually a metaphor for puberty." I paused to gauge their response to this epiphany but they remained stone faced. They were either true professionals or truly clueless. "Do you guys know what a metaphor is?"

"Yes, Mr. Marr. Let's move on, shall we? Number eight. When I don't get what I want, I often get unhappy."

"True. Especially sex. When I don't get sex I get very unhappy. And I have to admit I am in a bit of a dry spell. Fourteen years. So I guess you could say that I have been often unhappy in the last fourteen years. It seems like sex is a weird thing that used to happen to me sometimes."

"Number nine. I would like to fall in love and share my life with someone."

"True. Oh, very true. Falling in love can make you do strange things like brushing your teeth or showering. And I would love an excuse to manscape. Like, to truly manscape. As it stands right now, I have no real reason to trim my pubic hair into fun and amusing shapes. Also, I feel like my sense of humour could really wake a slumbering lady from her slumber!"

"And finally, number ten. My symptoms are the result of how I have conducted my life."

"False. I drink a litre of gin a day. And, at first, I thought the gin was sort of making me crazy. But I truly believe that what is making me crazy is my psychosis. My craziness, if you will."

At 3:17 pm the next afternoon, my olive green rotary dial vintage telephone rang. I skipped into the kitchen and answered somewhat cheerfully, expectantly.

"Hello?"

"Yes? Mr. Marr?" The voice said.

"Yes. Speaking. Thank you. How are you?"

"Fine, thanks. This is Dr. Galloway from the Department of Psychiatry at the Royal Vic."

"Yes! Dr. Galloway! I really enjoyed the conversation between myself and you and your colleague! I hope to have many more of these conversations in the very near future! And I meant to say, by the way, that you looked very fetching in that sweater!"

"Yes, well. Thanks for that. However, based our screening interview, it has been determined that you are not a suitable candidate for our cognitive therapy program."

"But," I said, "but ... I'm sad."

"I am sorry, Mr. Marr."

Since I was deemed to be an unsuitable candidate for cognitive therapy (which, by the way, is total fucking bullshit), I went to the Metro Montreal Medical Walk-in Clinic of Medicine in order to speak to a doctor about my lingering depression. It was only a walk-in clinic, but these practitioners had surely taken the same oath of Hippocrates as all doctors must!

Dr. Marwhani was a frail man with kind eyes. He asked me to pop off my shirt and take a seat on the examination table.

"You are a very fat man," Dr. Marwhani said.

"Yes sir, I'm a little overweight. Mildly overweight."

Dr. Marwhani cackled. "Oh! Please! My father is called sir! But my father is dead, so yes, indeed, call me sir. Or doctor. In any event, show me some respect!"

"Yes, Doctor."

"You need to eat much, much less."

"Yes, Doctor. But you see, my problem, I feel, is not primarily my weight."

"Hmm. Well it is no asset!"

"Right. Well I came here to see if you could do something for my sadness."

"Your sadness?"

"You see...I have not been with a sexual partner of any sort for fourteen years and..."

"Well, I can understand that. It seems dubious for a girl or sexual partner of any sort (as you put it) to fall for such an unattractive emotional eater. Perhaps you should stop thinking about it."

Finally, I snapped. Just a little. "Doctor. Could you please lay off the weight comments? They are hurting my feelings and making me angry. I'm here for anti-depressants. I want strong anti-depressants. The strongest you have."

"Fine. Here's what I will do. What's your name?" Dr. Marwhani looked down at his patient file. "Steven Marr. OK, Steven, I will take you on as my personal project. Do you have a family doctor?"

"No."

"You do now. It is me. Dr. Marwhani. I am your family doctor now." He began to scrawl on a prescription pad. "Here is a prescription for six months of Citalopram. And another for six months of Clonazepam. Come see me in six months on the nose. You will be a healthier person if you use these drugs to cure your sadness instead of always using pizza." Dr. Marwhani handed the prescription to me and then quickly snatched it back. "Also, let me add a six-month supply of Finasteride. It's for prostate health, but if you section the pill into quarters, you can use it to regrow hair! On your head! Isn't it delightful that the future is now? With luck, in six months, you will no longer be balding or obese! Then we will possibly see about getting you some sex with a brand new lady where you wouldn't even have to pay!"

I smiled a thankful smile and left the office and headed straight to the pharmacy.

The first week of reuptaking was an adventure in the surreal. I trudged through my routines, soy coffee stops, bookstore perusals. There was a different pitch to reality now. It was as though there was a vise tightening on my skull. It was as though God himself had taken two of his godly fingers and pinched my temples and just held on, guiding me through this oddly patterned existence. I felt like God's action figure. It felt urgent yet pleasant and very real. More real than any dream of realness I have ever known! I felt that I was amused and touched more than I ever had been and often by very simple things which were becoming stunningly beautiful, like chipmunks eating out of Doritos bags, or homeless men masturbating daintily behind very large, regal trees with weeping branches. I was growing accustomed to this new pressure that was being applied to my head and the small joys that accompanied it. It all felt right. Something very new and exciting was happening to me. I discovered that I had a desire to try new things; I discovered that I had the ability to follow through. And that's when I took up competitive eating.

#SWEETPROTIPS

Try to be more Christ-like. And by "Christ-like" I mean try having twelve eager men around you at all times.

"I'm gonna undo all that progress you and your therapist made" is a surprisingly effective pickup line.

If you whisper "I want to comb your hair so hard" to four people at the walk-in clinic, then your wait will be four people shorter!

If you hate your family, have Peter Gabriel's "Sledgehammer" played at your funeral.

Always look for ways to monetize your abjection.

You don't need to reach the end of the movie *Cocoon* because once you ejaculate, what's the point?

You can either go out in a blaze of glory or put on a blazer and go to a glory hole.

Chat Roulette is a wonderful way to reconnect with your high school principal and his penis!

If you fuck up a lot, say things like: "The most beautiful aspect of a Persian rug is always its deliberate flaw."

Whenever someone says, "Suck my dick," don't get too discouraged when you realize they don't mean it literally and you won't actually get to suck that dick.

Breaking up can be a difficult pill to swallow. But forty Klonopins are remarkably easy pills to swallow!

Writing is an adventure you go on with a ragtag team of misfits in search of treasure. No wait. That's *The Goonies*. Fuck. Sorry.

Connect with people through information superhighways such as the Internet.

It turns out that the best "safe word" is actually three words: "I love you."

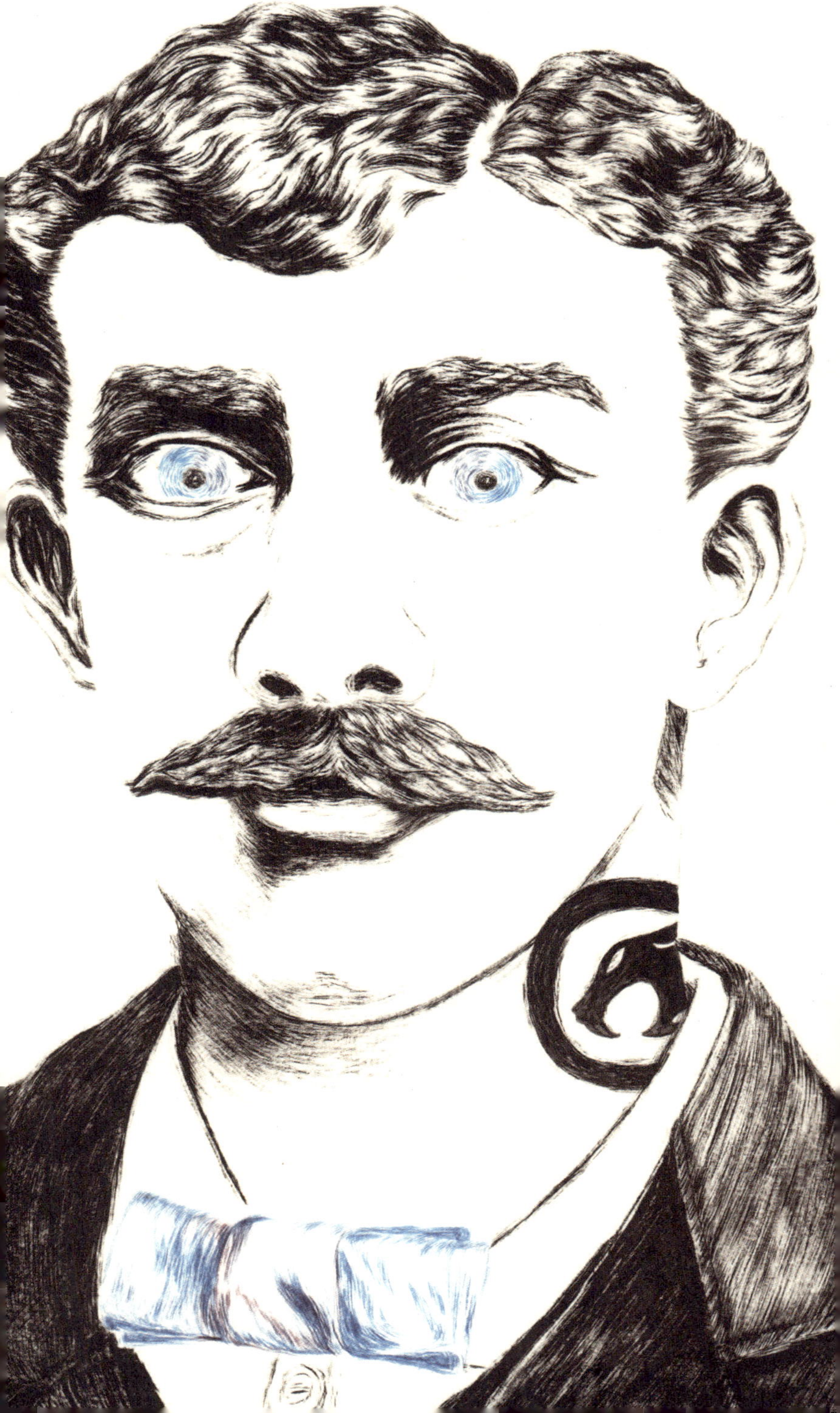

Never have sex while being sober. It's really weird.

One very effective way of getting out of a relationship is to never speak to that person ever again. Also moving far away. Also murdering them. You can do all three I guess.

Get a Thundercats neck tattoo!

There is no saying that will make you crave death more than the saying: "Live a little!"

Writing poetry should be its own reward. But if it isn't, at least you will get sweet royalty cheques.

If you really want to impress your sex worker, take him/her to a Holiday Inn Express!

If you are not feeling "literary" enough, try cigarettes. You will look and feel great and there's no downside!

If your sex life seems dull, try BDSM: Bathing, Diet Soda, and Manscaping!

CRITICAL THEORY ARCHIE

When I was a kid, my parents wouldn't buy me regular *Archie* comics. Instead, they provided me with every issue of Christian *Archie* comics. It occured to me recently that these proselytizing texts can be much improved by replacing the dialogue with phrases from seminal critical theory texts. So that's what I did.

THE LAUGH OF THE MEDUSA
I SHALL SPEAK ABOUT WOMEN'S WRITING: ABOUT WHAT IT WILL DO!!!!!!
THEIR STREAM OF.........
PHANTASMS IS INCREDIBLE
HERE
THEY ARE
RETURNING, ARRIVING OVER AND AGAIN

"YOU ONLY HAVE TO LOOK AT THE MEDUSA STRAIGHT ON TO SEE HER AND SHE'S NOT DEADLY. SHE'S BEAUTIFUL AND SHE'S LAUGHING." - HÉLÈNE CIXOUS

THE HISTORY OF SEXUALITY
IN POINT OF FACT
THE ASSERTION THAT SEX IS NOT
RE-PRESSED
IS NOT
NEW!! !!!!
WE MUST AT THE SAME TIME CONCEIVE OF SEX
WITHOUT THE LAW! !!!
POWER WITHOUT THE KING! !!!!!!!

POWER COMES FROM BELOW!
THERE IS NO BINARY!
THE HISTORY OF....
SEXUALITY SUPPOSES TWO RUPTURES
THE DARK SHIMMERS
OF SEX !!!!
WE MUST NOT REFER A HISTORY OF SEXUALITY TO THE AGENCY OF SEX !!!
THE DISCOURSE ON SEX HAS BEEN MULTIPLIED RATHER THAN RAREFIED!!!

LIFE IS DIFFICULT BUSINESS, PERRY

When I was turning from tween to teen, I had dreams of becoming a pop star. I fancied myself a kind of Neil Finn from Crowded House type — not entirely unattractive, pleasant, well-dressed, and seemingly attainable for the lonely ladies. I had an electric guitar, a cherry red fake Gretsch, and a few songs up my sleeve. At the age of fourteen, I had penned my first ballad: "Loneliness Is a Dirty Word." It had a Smiths vibe to it, but it was wholly my own. As I shuffled toward manhood, the songs became more sophisticated.

By the age of eighteen, I had penned such personal classics as "Heart Broker," "My Eldest Sister Is My Brother," and what I had projected to be my breakout hit single, the rockabilly-influenced, super jangly tune, "High Tea with Satan." I had no band, but I had a plan. I would be a solo artist. And I would go by the name Lamé. The accent on the e was an essential component of the name. It transformed what might be considered mundane and lame into a beautiful, shiny, risky word that challenged perceptions of gender.

I had kept up a lifelong correspondence with my slightly older cousin, Jasmine, who lived in Utica, New York. As tweens, we shared an affinity for magazines such as *Bop*, *Tiger Beat*, and *Seventeen*. Our twinned interests continued into our teens as we discovered the wonders of Tears for Fears, Crowded House, and Glass Tiger. Our cousinhood was strong and we considered each other kindred spirits.

In her early twenties, Jasmine had entered Film Studies at Columbia University and lived off-campus in nearby Harlem. I had nothing to live for in Winnipeg. I knew my dreams would die in Winnipeg and they would surely flourish in New York. I knew Jasmine would welcome me, at least as a temporary guest. After all, we were tethered like a tetherball to a tetherball pole! I would take these songs, my fake Gretsch, and seven of my favourite XL-sized lamé blouses of various colours to New York where I would fearlessly chase down my dream. I would be Lamé.

I fell in love for the first time. And it was the exciting new living situation with Jasmine that led to the discovery of

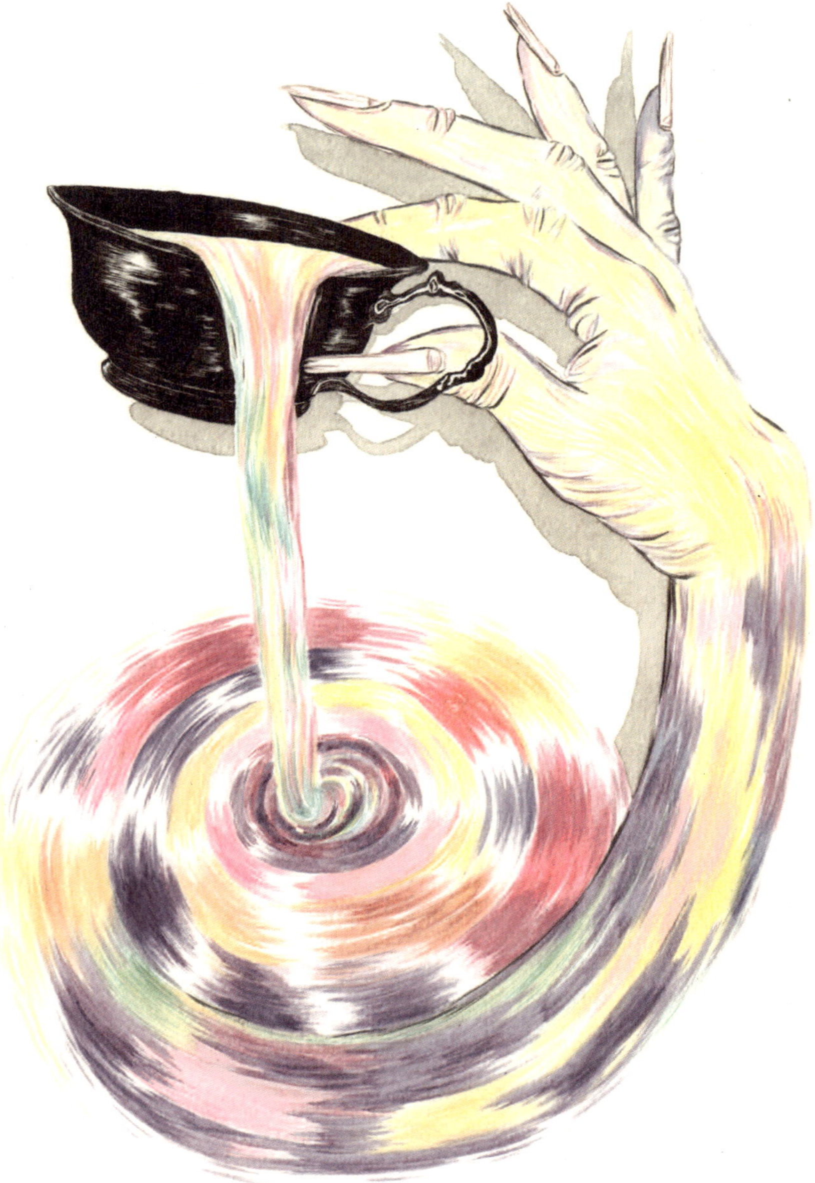

Perry. Perry was also an MA student in Film Studies and the teaching assistant for a class on propaganda film aesthetics that Jasmine was currently taking. They had become fast friends on account of their mutual love of marijuana and binge drinking. Perry: dark brown hair and eyes. Pixie cut. Jean jacket. Pinstriped baggy men's slacks. Checkered suspenders. Clash T-shirt — Combat Rock. She was neither masculine nor feminine. She was unique. Genderless. Like I had always thought God probably was if God existed but she/he didn't. Perry. There was only one Perry.

In this moment I felt like I was in a poem. Something like "A Supermarket in California" except in Harlem and I was not into other dudes. As Jasmine and Perry made small chit-chat about the aesthetic value of *The Triumph of the Will*, I was moved to speak to this woman, this vision, this fancy graduate-level angel.

"Do you like Allen Ginsberg?" I blurted, at a volume of eleven.

"Alex! Don't interrupt," Jasmine snarked.

"What?" asked Perry.

"Sorry. Umm...do you like Allen Ginsberg? 'Cause he's like, uh, one of my favourite poets and I'm, like, writing a song, because I'm a songwriter, and it's sort of based on a poem of his that is set in a grocery store and is very beautiful, the poem I mean, although the song's alright too. It's kind of got a Roxy Music vibe to it but with a tinge of Peter Gabriel, the good stuff of Gabriel's, you know. Like 'Sledgehammer.' Anyway, that poem is in a grocery store, just like us! We are in a grocery store too! Right?"

Jasmine looked at Perry with eyes that simultaneously said, "I'm sorry" and "What the fuck?"

"Yeah, Ginsberg is OK. But, like, wasn't he a member of NAMBLA or something?" Perry asked.

"Oh, probably! He was probably very, very smart."

"Right," Perry said, laughing.

"You're thinking of MENSA, Alex," Jasmine said.

I did not miss a beat. I remained fixated on Perry. I couldn't help but spill everything that could possibly be surveyed in the landscape of my grey matter. "Do you like Gowan? He's a Canadian singer. Maybe he's not known here but he will be. Very cool, very cool stuff. Do you have a boyfriend? Are you originally from Harlem or Manhattan or something? Do you like strawberry sundaes? I play guitar at the Ninety-Sixth Street station every day. You know, just busking for cash and stuff. I have a sweet guitar. Cherry red Gretsch. Not a real Gretsch, but it looks just like one and it has f-holes. Do you like f-holes? Most people like f-holes. What's your favourite OMD song?"

Perry laughed a bit more. "You're sweet and super ridiculous," she said.

Jasmine yanked me by the sleeve of my army green cardigan. "Listen, Alex. You can make yourself useful, OK? There's a party tonight on Amsterdam Avenue. You're totally invited. But you got to get to the health food store. Here's sixty. Go get, like, two bags of the indoor stuff and meet me back at home OK? I will grab the beer."

"OK. Cool." I turned once more to Perry and said, again too loud, "I'm going to purchase some drugs for us. We'll do them later together, OK?

The girls hurried down the aisle clutching each other's jackets and whispering.

The party was intimidating, even after one joint and three cans of Pabst Blue Ribbon. I hovered around the periphery. A sea of plaid, vintage jeans, bandanas — of goatees, wizard beards, chin straps — of nose rings, tattoos, ironic makeup. From the dreadlocked to the finely coiffed, the students of Columbia's arts community were simply out of social reach. Perry smiled politely at me; Jasmine bounced her way toward a graduate student dude with thick pork chop sideburns and a ratty Vans T-shirt. There was a level of discourse that seemed unattainable to me. There were vaguely familiar name drops: Deleuze and Guattari, Butler, Foucault, Derrida. There were terms bandied about like shuttlecocks: "Hegemony," "Phallocentrism," "Phallogo-

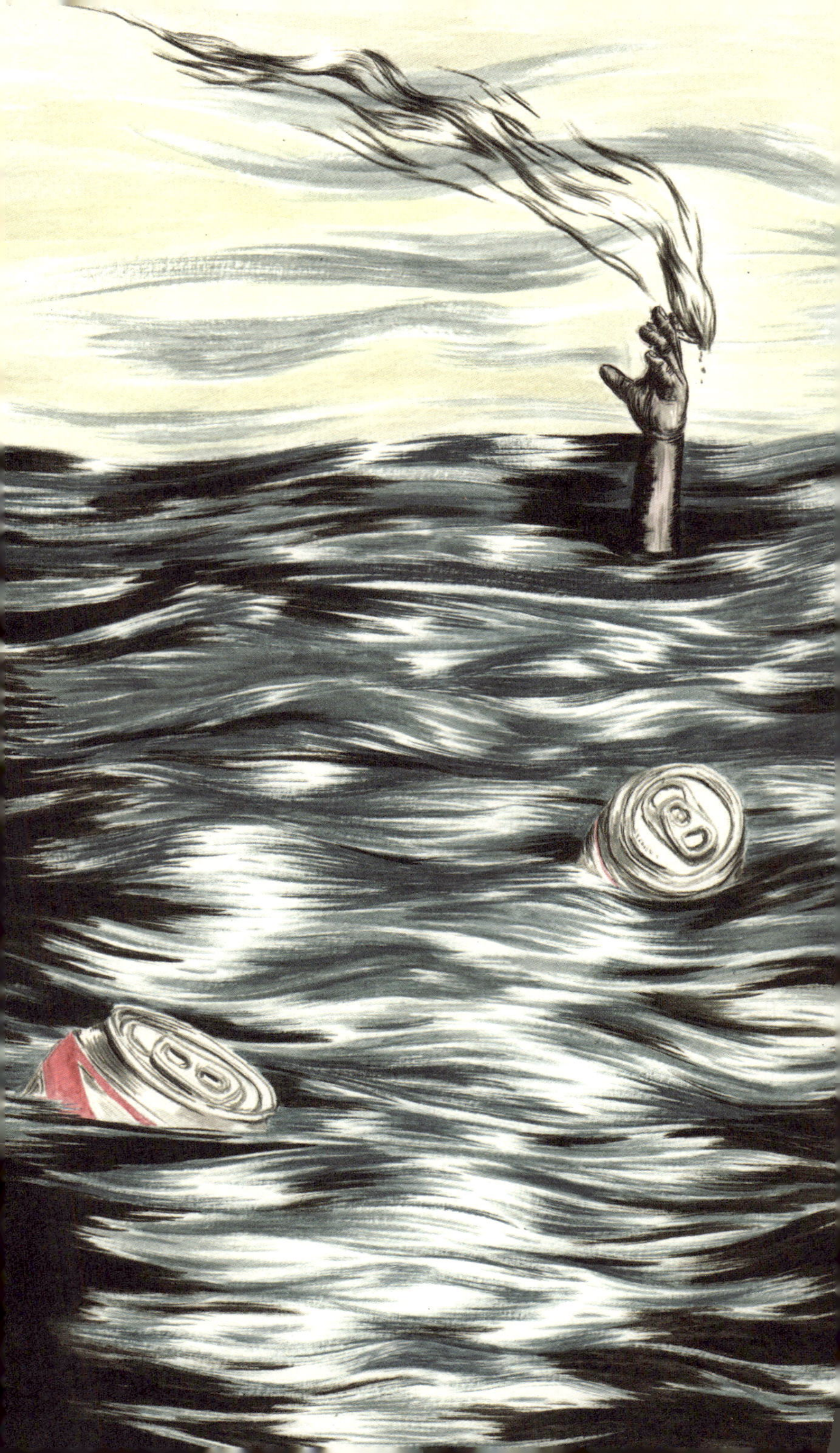

centrism," "Interpellation!" Instead of risking embarrassment, I reminded myself of my failure at the grocery store, and remained quiet, cool, content. I nodded my head to the Counting Crows, even though I had always despised them.

The trick of surviving a grad school party is to just be cool. To not make waves. To look like you belong and it's all good. This is what I kept telling myself. I glanced over at Perry but also gave her distance. As long as I had a beer in my hand and my wits about me, there was going to be a moment when we would speak and Perry would come to realize the connection that was so clearly there.

As I feigned interest in a slurry speech about Russian formalism by some guy in a hemp sweater with a bright green bead in his straggly goatee, I met eyes with Perry who smiled and gave me the international signal for "let's smoke a joint!" I darted over, mid-Russian formalism speech, and followed Perry out to the balcony. It was a humid spring night and I was sweating more than a healthy young man should. I wiped my brow and watched as Perry expertly rolled a joint on her lap.

"Hot night, eh?" I said.

"Not really. I'm kinda chilly."

"Me too!"

Perry sighed. "Uh-huh? Well you're sweating a tonne."

"Oh yeah? It's my diabetes."

"You have diabetes?"

"Probably. Or maybe I'm just nervous."

"Yeah. Why are you like this? You seem like a normal kid. But then you are psycho-frantic, or withdrawn and weird. What is your story, anyway?"

Normal kid. Those two words simultaneously made my blood boil and anxiety heighten. "I'm not a kid. And I'm proud to not be normal. Normal is lame. And I'm *Lamé*. I'm an artist and, I must confess, I'm a little tortured. I had a very difficult upbringing. What I mean is that I was abused, sort of. That is to say, at least not treated well. I have some things to work through and I plan on doing that. I plan on working through things with my music and whatnot." At this point, I was sweating so profusely that I resembled a some sort of sea creature with a glandular problem. "Life is difficult business, Perry. That's why I recently wrote this new power ballad called "Life Is Difficult Business, Perry" and I would love to sing it for you sometime soon. Frankly, I am doing my best to face what we have in front of us. I will be damned if I were to somehow not honour this thing, this special thing that we could have, that we *do* have if only you would open your eyes to this thing which is clearly love!"

"What the fuck are you talking about?" Perry said,

handing me the joint and a tissue. "First off, there is no way in hell we could ever hook up. You're kind of cute, but you are a child! I date *men* and *women*, not *children*. Jesus Christ! And secondly, *everyone* has had a fucked up childhood. Everyone. It's so boring. Like, who cares? Get over it and grow up...kid!"

I rolled my eyes, wiped my brow with the tissue and handed it back to Perry, who grimaced and dropped it. I just stood there. I tried to remain composed. I tried to take it in stride. To grow up. Instantly. Right there. On the spot. Grow up, Alex. Grow up now. Instead, my lower lip quivered and then I cried. I sobbed. I wailed and tore through the incense-drenched apartment and spilled out onto the street.

On Morningside Drive, Jasmine found me slumped over in a phone booth.

"Hey, cuz, it's not safe out here this time of night," Jasmine said.

"I'm alright."

"That was quite a scene back there. You sure you're good?"

"Did people laugh at me?"

"Oh yeah! Pretty much everyone. It was pretty hilarious. You have this weird thing when you cry. You look like a manatee with a glandular problem. And you make this noise, sorta like a screech, but even higher pitched. It's, well, just weird. And super funny. People were trying to do impressions of it, but it's so hard to do! It's like not even a human sound. It's like a fucked up mating call or something. Maaaaaaaayah! Maaaaaaaaayah! Oh I can't do it now! I totally had it down like five minutes ago. Ha! Anyways. They're all calling you 'Manatee Boy' now."

"Oh, God."

"Listen, cuz. Maybe you should go back to Winnipeg soon. I think you might be a bit in over your head here."

"But...I don't want to."

"I think it may be best." Jasmine reached out her hand and pulled me up onto my feet. "Think about it. Here. Take my key. I'm gonna get back to the party. Just buzz me in when I get back, OK? Love you cuz."

"I love you, too."

I rifled through Jasmine's desk and found her address book. I located Perry's phone number and dialed.

"Hello?" It was a man's voice.

"Is Perry there?"

"No. She's out. Can I take a message?"

"Yes. Yes you can. But it will be quite long. Do you have a good pen, a pad of paper and around twenty or so minutes?"

The man hung up. I called again and this time, the answering machine picked up. It was Perry's voice. "Hello. You've reached Simon, David, Sparkle, and Perry. Leave a message!"

And so I left a message. "Perry, it's Alex. I am a little drunk, to be sure. I drank some Chinese cooking wine that I found in Jasmine's kitchen. It was pretty OK. And listen, I need to express, for the first and possibly last time, that you have destroyed me but I will rebuild myself. I am a human, grown-up *man*, Perry. Just like you. A man's man among men. Except you are a lady. A man's lady. And God knows I've never truly humped a lady, but I know that I would be just fantastic at it. Listen Perry, if that is your real name, Perry, I'm totally good at fucking. I can just feel it in my bones. I mean, people look at me and probably think, that dude is too lame to be good at fucking. And he probably cries like a weird half-man/half-manatee. But that's so very wrong to assume and so fuck all of those people. I mean, it's weird, me telling you this when you were so very cruel to me tonight. How can someone who likes Allen Ginsberg and is artistic-looking and so pretty also be so mean? I mean, I mean, I was hoping and willing and planning on giving you my very first virginity. So what I'm saying is that if you gave me some minutes to love you I would still say yes. Still, despite your cruelty, I know if you change your heart and mind, I would make you explode with happiness and sexual fulfillment. Absolutely explode, Perry. Absolutely explode. Just like my exploded heart. Which is the name of my new song I am writing right now, as we speak."

I hung up. From then on, my music took on a whole new life. I moved back home, found some like-minded individuals, and formed a prog-rock band: Protoplasthma. You know the rest of the story.

THE PARABLE
OF BRYAN DONG

This is the parable of Bryan Dong. It is somewhat parabolic. Back in the day, in a very specific suburb of Winnipeg, specifically Transcona, when I was an elementary school student, from the age of six, I used to go to Bryan Dong's house every weekday for lunch. I was a latchkey kid. Bryan was the greatest person in the world. I was perfectly aware that I sometimes annoyed Bryan. It was hard not to be somewhat overenthusiastic in Bryan's presence. I felt a real sense of dedication to my best friend. Not only was Bryan one of the most popular and physically attractive boys at Harold Hatcher Elementary School, but his parents, Roy and Deandra, were the Block Parents of Allenby Crescent. Every decent street in Winnipeg had a house that was designated the Block Parent home. If a child were to be in danger of any kind, they could find safety and solace in the arms of a Block Parent. I felt especially lucky that my mom had brokered the lunchtime deal with Mrs. Dong. Not only did it result in what I was sure would be a deep, lifelong friendship, it was also the best possible scenario in terms of safety. I worried about the black vans with tinted windows, the leather-jacketed, mustachioed loners that seemed to linger around the school at recess and after 3:30 pm. I had an acute sense of security about the whole thing. And I had an even more acute affection for Bryan Dong.

Bryan played hockey. Bryan was popular. Bryan dragged me into the basement to make him bang on pots and pans to Boney M. and Queen songs. I would always keep a faithful beat as Bryan crooned "Another One Bites the Dust" or "Rivers of Babylon." I once told Bryan that I considered him to be my best friend and that sometimes I would lie in bed at night and close my eyes and imagine the next time we would play together. Bryan said nothing, just sat there cross-legged and brushed neon orange Doritos seasoning from the crotch of his jeans. Bryan was stoic as shit.

During our lunch hours, I would cross my legs, attempting the same pose that Bryan had perfected, and eat macaroni and cheese and watch *Spiderman* cartoons. When *Spiderman* was over, we would watch the first twenty or so minutes of a thirty-minute kids' show, *Uncle*

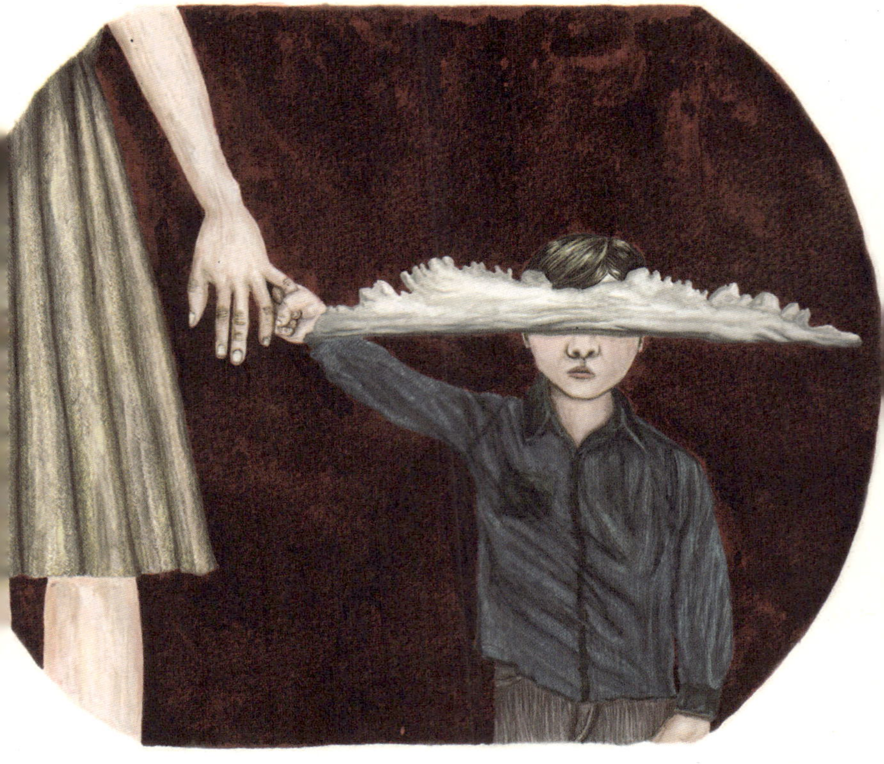

Archie and also Neil and Bob. This particular show was hosted by an old dude, Uncle Archie, who was accompanied by his two puppets, Neil and Bob, who provided Winnipeg-specific commentary on the Winnipeg Jets, the Winnipeg Blue Bombers, the Rotary Club, and the Shriners. I was captivated by this spectacle and would do my best to hold on to the lunch hour. Oh, Uncle Archie.

I hung on every slurry word. I would do my best to linger until the end of the show, when he would hold up a prop hand-held mirror with candy-red trim and an empty space where the mirror should be and peer through it. Then he would call out the names of all the special boys and girls he could see out there in their living rooms. I would concentrate as hard as possible on Uncle Archie's kindly, wrinkled face, his tobacco-stained teeth, his bloodshot eyes. I would try to make eye contact with Uncle Archie, desperate to be named. Bryan was named at least once a week. For me, it only happened once: I was purposefully repacking my *GoBots* backpack slowly, stalling. Uncle Archie lifted the hollow mirror to his face and gazed directly at the camera lens which was me. Bryan had already made his way to the front entrance where he was velcroing his shoes. "I see so many wonderful children out there, all of my special friends: I see Jeffery, Bradley, John, Matthew, Brittany, Kenneth, and Bryan! And I see you too, special

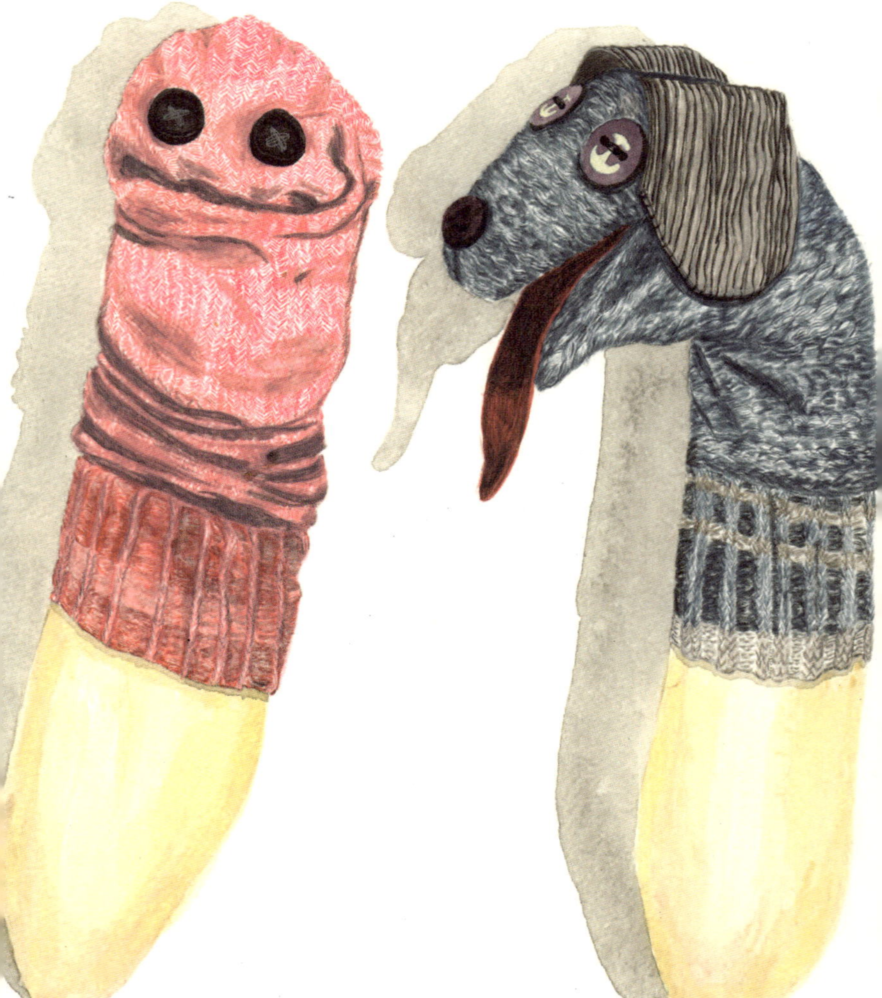

friend." I gasped and felt a jolt of something I had never felt before. Some sort of swelling. I think it was a swelling of pride.

"Bryan! Did you here that? Uncle Archie saw us! Both of us! He said Kenneth!"

"Big deal!" Bryan said, "He always sees me."

"It is a big deal to me!"

"Whatever."

The next morning, before school, my mother pulled me aside.

"Kenneth, today you will be having lunch at Vance Sawatsky's house."

"What? Vance Sawatsky is the worst — the absolute worst kid in school, Mom. He is so much the worst that his nickname is 'The Worst!' Bryan is my lunch buddy. He is my one and only lunch buddy!"

"Not anymore, dear. Now shut your trap, and off you go."

I sighed and rolled my eyes. I was at a loss. I trudged to school at a slower-than-usual pace. The air was crisp and asthmatic and the leaves were changing. I booted little gravel stones and choked on the dust they kicked up. What had happened? Why was I being torn away from the one person who mattered? As I entered Harold Hatcher Elementary School, I knew that I had to see Bryan as soon as possible and tell him. Bryan would be so disappointed.

The cloakroom was empty except for Bryan and me. I reached out to touch Bryan's hand. Bryan recoiled.

"So, before we hit the monkey bars, I need to tell you something. My big dumb mother won't let me come to your place for lunch. What the heck, hey?"

"Yeah, Kenneth. I think that's probably a good thing."

"I don't ... I don't understand."

"Kenneth. You are a good guy and stuff, but I feel that we should move on."

"Move on?"

"I don't want to be your friend."

"But you're my best and only friend! Why are you doing this?"

"Kenneth. I'm just going to say this once. You are emotionally needy. Like, way too needy. It's too much for me to take."

"What does that mean? We're only ten years old, Bryan. Those are grown-up words."

"Well, I guess I'm just a grown-up then." With that, Bryan Dong left me alone in the cloakroom. I slumped to the floor, buried my face in my *GoBots* backpack, and wept.

As the days became shorter and the fall grew colder, I was

more and more withdrawn. I went for long walks after school, exploring the ditches and abandoned lots and cars of Transcona. I felt no need to report to dinner on time, to adhere to any familial imperatives. I was searching for something. Something about myself. I needed to find a way to be less needy. To be more likeable.

One late afternoon, I was rummaging through the sticky backseat of an abandoned 1980 Dodge Dart in the southwest corner of a small field swathed in prairie tall grass, when I saw a black van with tinted windows slowly making its way down Redonda Street. I sat, hunched over in the backseat, motionless, hoping to not be noticed. But the black van kept swinging back around, creeping up and down the street. I clenched my fists; I saw my breath in the air. I decided I had to head home like a bastard. But I told myself to be casual. To walk swiftly, but not to look panicked. I began to march through the tall grass and toward my home. I made it to the back lane of Allenby Crescent. The black van turned off Redonda and down the lane, still crawling along, but gaining on me. I quickened my pace to a brisk jog. The van adjusted its speed accordingly. I was now behind the Dong home. *Block Parent*! *Block Parent*! I zigged toward the back door of the safe house. And, almost as quickly, I zagged back to the lane. *Emotionally needy*! *Emotionally needy*! I swore to God I

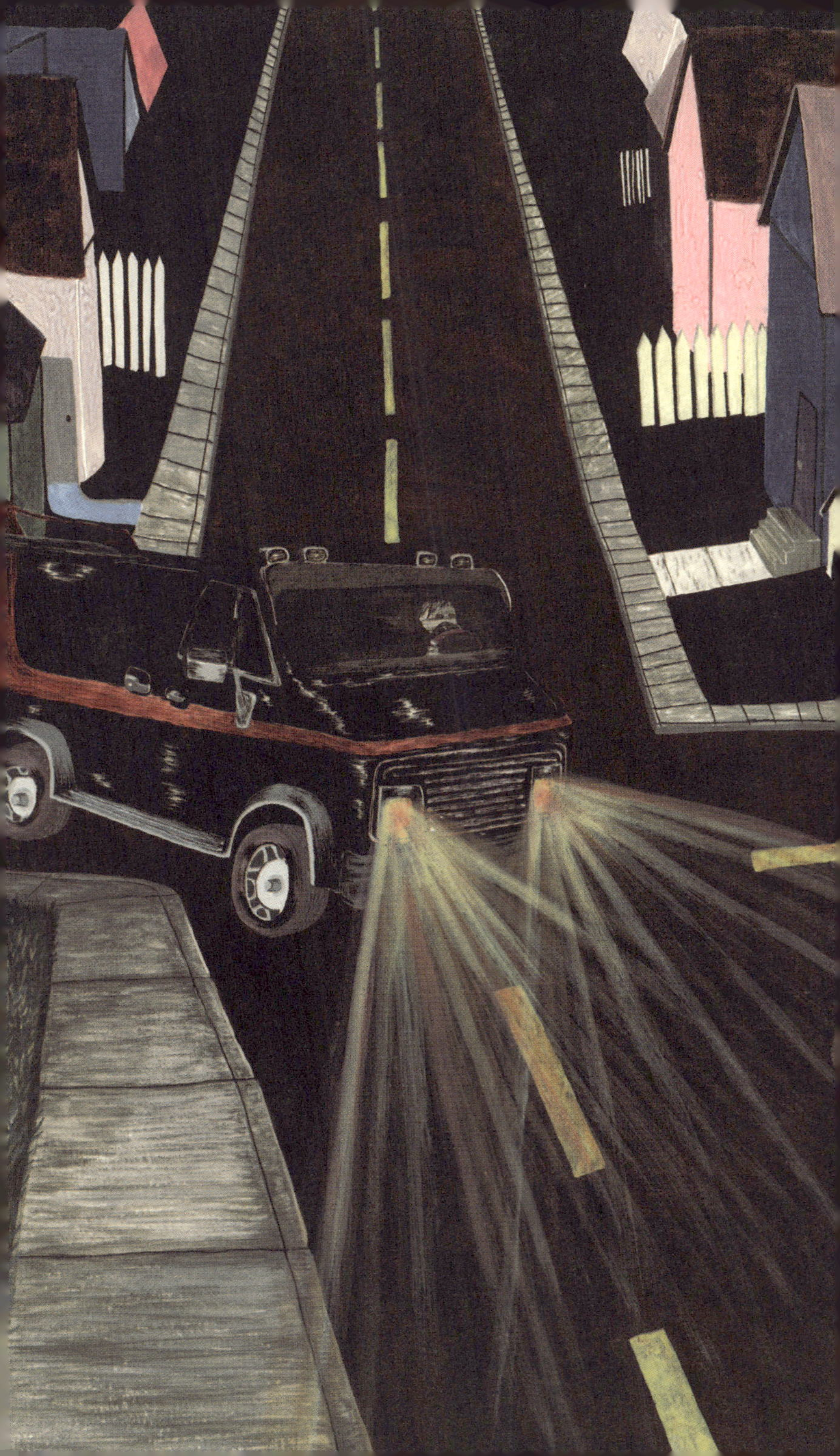

would rather be chopped into a thousand pieces and have those pieces sold to perverts from around the world through some kind of intricate black market mail-order type system than be seen as *emotionally needy* in the eyes of the Dongs once more! I quickened to a sprint as the van's high beams enveloped me. I bolted home as fast as my underdeveloped legs could take me and I almost made it, too.

INVIGILATOR

Montreal University. Downtown Campus. Annex B, fifth floor. Winter semester. You lock eyes with fresh-faced, bright-eyed undergraduates. Some of them are cheaters. You know this on account of all of your experiences with cheating. You had never cheated at anything, but you have a great deal of experience with the cheating of cheaters. That's for sure.

The students look at you with varying degrees of disdain, reverence, and desire. You recently took out a book from the Montreal University library on the topic of pedagogy and desire. It's called *Pedagogy and Desire* and it explains that the "subject presumed to know" (that is you) "was always cast in the role of the desired and highly sexualized figure." (You totally get that.) It is argued in the book that: "the pedagogue, with his alpha status, and his unquestionable potency, must be ever-vigilant to guard against the tacit and explicit advances of the young, female (and occasional male) scholar." You have never experienced the psychosexual thrust, so to speak, of an explicit advance, but you are very well aware of all the unspoken, unsubstantiated, very subtle attention you are receiving. And, it is true, you are not technically a pedagogue, but you do have a kind of authority that makes you pedagogical in an immediate sense. And since you are in a position of such authority, it is inevitable that the hopes, dreams, and fantasies of young, post-pubescent, hyper-hormonal undergraduate students will fall upon you. It doesn't matter that you have never entirely rid yourself of your baby fat; it matters not that you are missing two molars and one incisor, or that your slightly graying hair is slowly receding despite your religious, liberal application of Rogaine.

The book tells you that you are inevitable fantasy material to these young women. And you believe the book. The book is so smart. And who are you to argue with a book? And so, you rue the day that you will have to break a young person's heart. But that day is sure to come, as sure as exams come thrice a year. And if you're honest with yourself, you look forward to it too. It would be one of those instances of "condolulations" which is a word you made up, combining "congratulations" and "condolences." Constructing neologistic portmanteaus is a habit of yours. It is your fifteenth year as an invigilator and, earlier this year, during the fall semester exams, your colleagues commemorated the milestone, as per your collective agreement, with a gift certificate to the agreed-upon restaurant, Mike's. You had the mozzarella sticks and a salad (which were the only vegetarian options) and three daiquiris. You got very emotional during your thank-you speech, and you felt that you had ruined the moment with unnecessary tears, tears you tried to hide by claiming that you were simply sweating from your eyes.

Later, at home, you throw yourself a private party for one. You buy fifteen vanilla cupcakes with sprinkles, some expensive red wine and an adult video. You stay up until 4 in the morning with the cupcakes and the video. Then a strange feeling overwhelms you. You feel crippling remorse and anxiety. You wrap the DVD and four cupcakes in your soiled bed sheets and place everything in a garbage bag and take it way down the street and place it in the dumpster behind the Italian restaurant so your roommate, the very perfect Sally, won't find anything. You are very careful about everything. Especially when it comes to invigilation and Sally.

Sally is an international student from rural Australia who had originally intended on studying chemistry. But when she arrived in the city and began living a cosmopolitan life, she began to experiment sexually with people, smoking marijuana, drinking alcohol, and, as a result, she switched her major to art history. You don't entirely approve of her life choices but you consider yourself a man of the world and a relativistic thinker. And some nights when Sally has a gentleman caller over for a rousing session of sexual congress, you press your ear to the wall — you and Sally have adjacent rooms — and you listen to the two of them and you "pound it" (as they say) to the sounds. Sally has a tendency to yelp like a frothing taser victim during sex, and as she is about to climax, she utters strange phrases like, "It's so big that you're knocking on the door of my cervix!" or "Your dick is my gateway drug!" You sometimes turn flaccid at the more peculiar phrases, but more often than not, you are turned on. In the two years she has been here, Sally has really become a true North American in your opinion. She has also gained weight, which is less of an opinion and more of a fact. It would be good for her, you sometimes muse, for her family to fetch her upon graduation so that she would have to return to her homeland and enter into one of those traditional Australian arranged marriages. But more often than not, you resist that thought. Sally has become special to you and it would be hard to let her go.

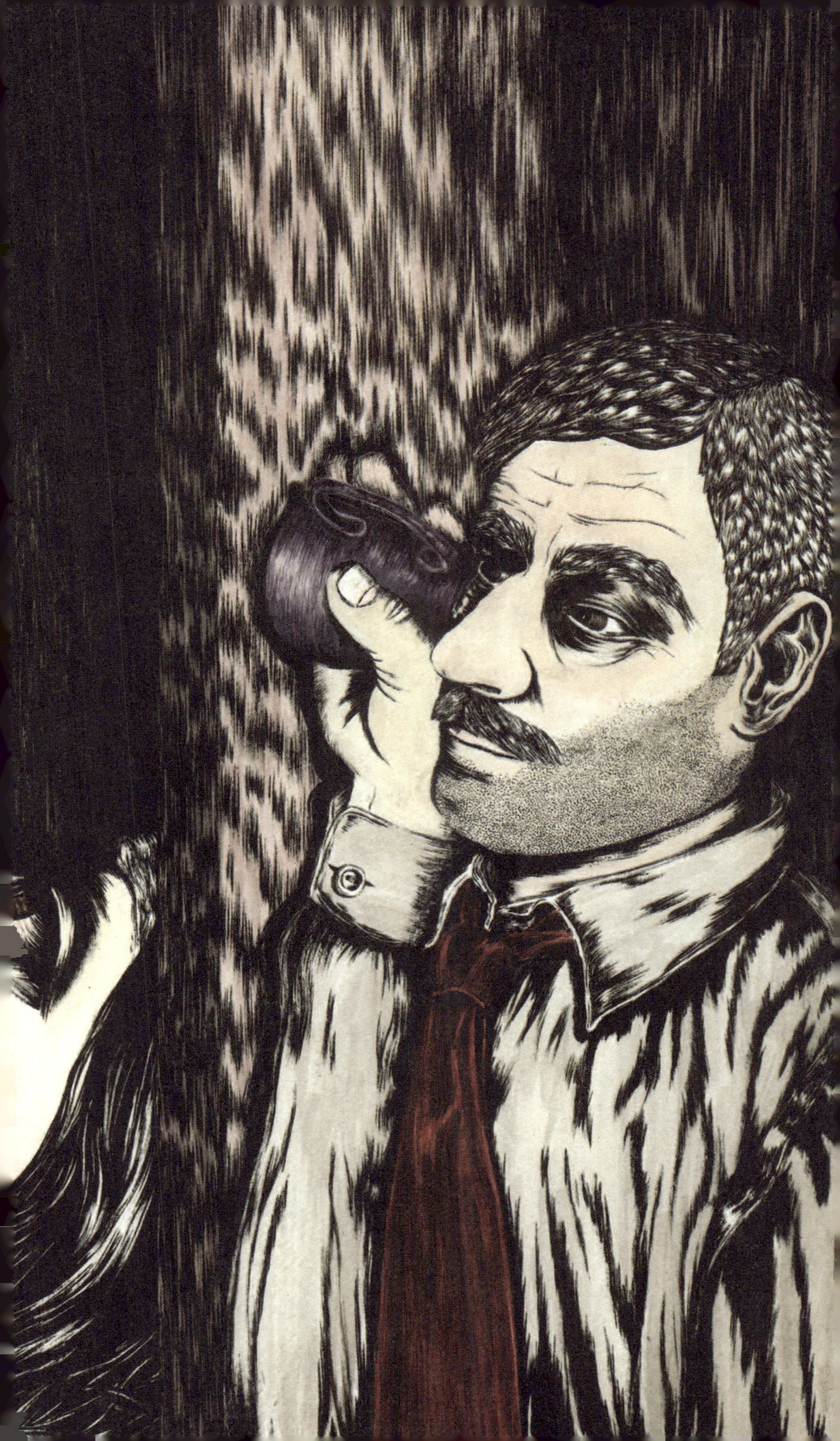

The winter semester is at a close and it is time for serious proctoring action. You are ready to invigilate. The first day of exams includes Introductory Accountancy, English Rhetoric and Composition, and Statistics. You are to be the head invigilator for the English exams and the alternate head invigilator for the others. The most senior of invigilators is Doyle. Doyle Morrow. Doyle has been working for twenty years. That is five more than you. But, still, you feel that there is a silent understanding among your confreres that you are the true veteran. You feel that you had a natural authority and a certain *je ne sais quoi* that is hard to put into words. Who knows what it is, frankly, but it is there because you feel it all the time in your head, in your heart, and it is yours and they know it and probably know that you know it also. That's why, although occasionally you get jealous of Doyle's hours and wage, you, for the most part, are easy-going about micropolitics.

Sally is scheduled to take her English Composition exam on a Wednesday and you are pleased because you want to champion her as she so richly deserves. You will be able to peek in on her particular classroom because you will be the head invigilator that day. You won't break from protocol, except to maybe give Sally a quick wink or thumbs up. That's an acceptable breach of professionalism. As for the room assignment, Doyle is the best choice to supervise Sally's class. Although he lacks the air of authority and the *je ne sais quoi* of a true leader, he is fair. Sally will be in good hands. You are aware that this will be the final exam of Sally's university career. She will soon be a bona-fide Art Historian, with a Bachelor of Arts and everything.

Sally approaches you in the kitchen on the eve of her composition exam. "I'm mighty nervous," she says, in an unfamiliar, timid voice.

"There is nothing to worry about, Sally. Your North American English has improved. Especially your idioms. I listen to you sometimes, you know."

"What do you mean?"

"Well, I hear you say things. And, often they are very close to normal English in their cadence and execution and, I must confess, it does get me excited sometimes."

"Well, thanks, I guess."

"And listen: I will not have the privilege of proctoring you myself…"

"What?"

"Oh, I suppose that sounds dirty. But it's not. Proctor is another word for invigilate! I have assigned my colleague Doyle Morrow to oversee the exam proceedings and he is a very competent invigilator in his own right. He will ensure that an environment of fairness and tranquility is preserved. Tell him you are my friend. He will give you a good desk."

"Oh. Right. Sure. Thanks. Whatever."

Sally enters the room fifteen minutes early and places two sharpened pencils and her student ID on her desk. When the exam arrives she looks over the essay questions:

Choose one of the following essay topics below. Write an essay of no more than 1500 words.

1. In your opinion, have celebrities gone too far in this day and age?
2. What is your favourite animal and why?
3. Do you believe that parents have the God-given right to beat their children?
4. Computers are an essential part of daily life: discuss.

Sally takes a deep breath, selects her topic, and formulates her essay title: "Beating Children: A Necessary Evil." Things are going quite well. She develops a thesis, three topic sentences and a conclusion. As well, she constructs a thought bubble in order to expand her ideas. She is halfway through her rough draft when she sees you at the door. You hold up a sign against the window of the door that says, "I

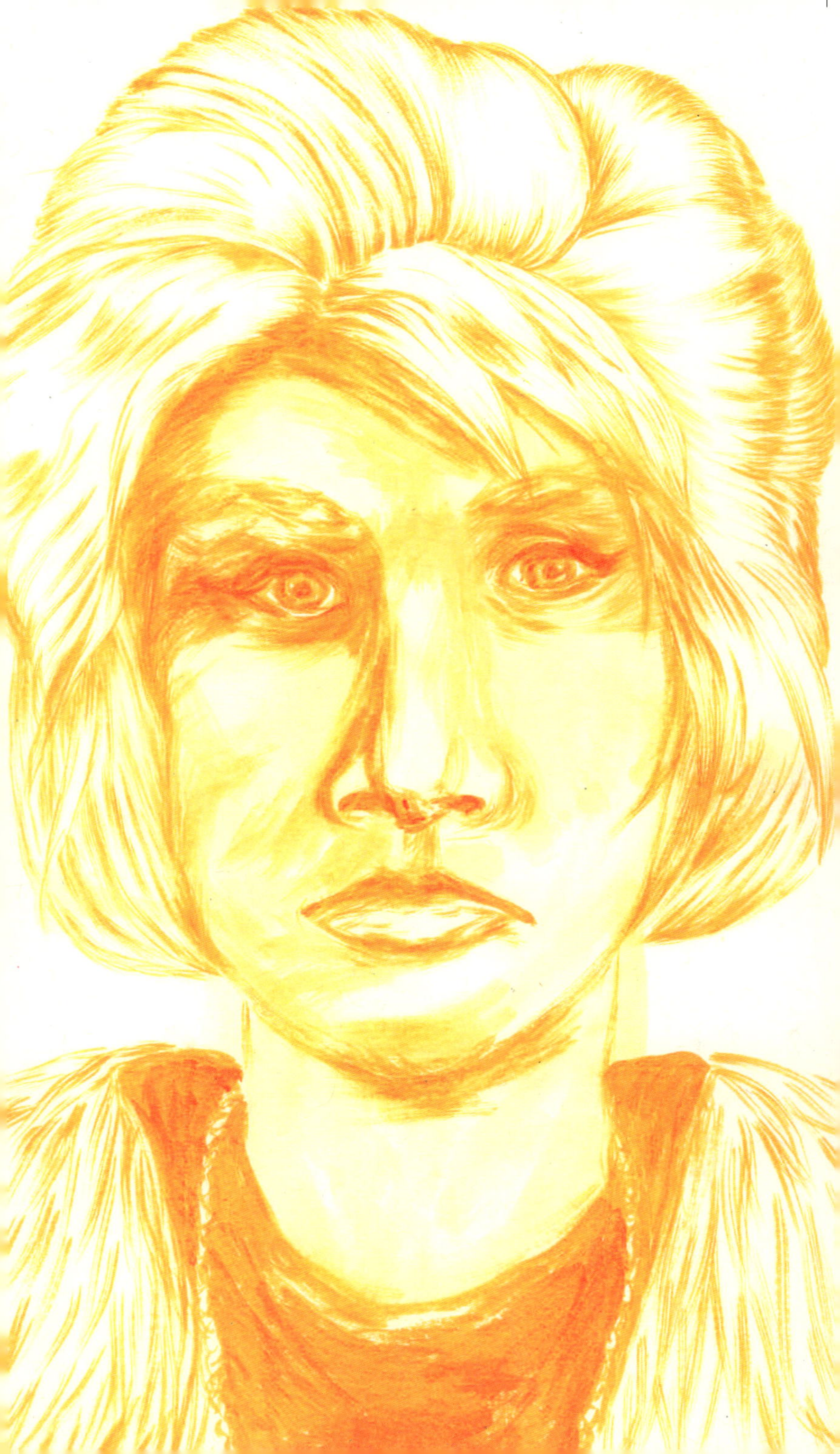

believe in you." You take down the sign, wink at Sally and give her a thumbs-up. When Sally smiles and reciprocates the thumbs-up, Doyle Morrow furrows his brow. "Excuse me, young lady."

"Oh…sorry. It was just my friend. You know him," Sally says, as the entire class turns to look at the door where you sheepishly grin and smile at Morrow.

"OK. Everyone settle down," Morrow says and glares at you.

The students go back to writing the exam and Morrow goes back to his *New York Times*. All seems to be settled, when the silence is broken by the tune of Beyonce's 2009 hit single, "Single Ladies (Put a Ring on It)." The unmistakable ring tone is coming from the breast pocket of Sally's pinstriped power suit. Sally grabs her cell phone and fumbles around with it. Eventually sending the incoming call to voice mail and silencing her phone. But the damage is done. Doyle Morrow is towering over her with a look of utter contempt in his eyes. "Young lady, were you not aware of the regulations forbidding electronic devices such as cell phones and electronic dictionaries from being on your person during the writing of this exam?"

"I'm so super sorry. I just forgot it. I should have handed it in."

"You bet your sweet academic career you should have handed it in. Give me your exam booklet."

"But, sir, it wasn't intentional."

"For all I know, that cell phone is equipped with a translation device and electronic text generator capabilities."

"No, sir. It's just a standard Nokia flip phone!"

"Give the booklet to me now!"

Sally hands her almost complete exam to Doyle Morrow and watches, helplessly, as he tears it up in front of everyone. There is a collective, muted gasp in the room. Sally begins to tear up and bolts from the room. The tears keep streaming as Sally weaves her way through the slush and sludge of the downtown Montreal streets toward home. She throws herself on her bed and after a lengthy session of snorting and bawling, she flips open her phone and checks her voice mail: "Hi Sally, it's me. I am calling from a payphone down the hall. I just wanted to apologize for my inelegant show of support today. I trust that you will get this message after you have successfully completed your exam and that you will forgive me. I do believe in you and I will not apologize for that sentiment. Proud of you!"

The exam season is now over and you receive a reprimand for fraternizing with a student and a year-long suspension. You are very much emotionally distraught by this and also by Sally's academic suspension and the corresponding emotional fallout. To top it all off, Sally's family has called for her. And Sally's spirits are so low, her future so bleak, that she has already printed out her ticket and packed her bags. You decide to take this year as a chance to take inventory and live on social assistance.

You twin Sally's moping about the apartment, and make sad eyes at her. Sally says she forgives you, but has no desire to speak to you at any length or in any depth. And it is clear she has no desire to rekindle the mild tolerant banter she once had afforded you. She says there is no time, no point.

One spring night, you slip into Sally's room with remarkable stealth and tap her on the shoulder. Sally gasps and scurries to the far corner of her bed. A slim, scraggly, undergraduate boy darts from the room, clutching his jeans and T-shirt. Sally cries out after him, "Donny!" But he is gone.

"I'm sorry, Sally. I'm sorry about everything."

"Jesus! What are you doing? What do you want?"

"I want your happiness. I mean, sorry, I want you to be happy. Again. Once more."

"Sigh."

"OK, Sally, but I've been thinking this over. Since, you know, you got suspended, and you got deported and stuff."

"I haven't been deported. I'm just going home."

"Right. Yeah. Well it's not right. And I will not have it."

"What do you propose to do?"

You get down on one knee in front of her bed. "Propose is the perfect word."

"Oh shit. No. Don't…"

"Sally, we have known each other since you answered my craigslist posting and then said you weren't interested but then moved in after that better place fell through. And in that time, I have grown to love you in a specific way. Specifically, I think you are a lady who is smart and has talents that are mostly sexual in nature from what I have heard and also you are, on a personal note, a nice person with social skills that are beyond my abilities. And you dress well for someone who wasn't born here and is now heavy-set. And listen, I can't promise you a perfect union. But I do promise that you can still fool around with all those other men and you can still go out and get drunk with your classmates if ever your suspension is to be lifted, and I truly believe it will be. And also, if you marry me, you will get citizenship. And then you can divorce me after a suitable amount of time if you do not, that is, learn to love me, which you might. So now that you have heard my proposal, let me show you the ring." You reach into your pocket and produce a jewellery box with a fairly impressive gold-plated ring with a cubic zirconium stone. "I got it from Sears!"

"Oh, Russell," Sally says, tears streaming down. And then she leaves the room and you don't see her again.

Your name is Russell. You hate it.

THE PROBLEM WITH LESLIE

From the moment I entered the world, I have had an eye-rolling problem. The story of my birth is the go-to tale of my father, John, at family gatherings and when he is binge drinking and therefore I have a keen sense how it all went down.

In the surprisingly dingy maternity ward of the Concordia Hospital, my parents, John and Meredith Mackie, held their "happy accident" — a "wrinkled little wretch of a human being." Almost genderless on account of my remarkably small penis and unremarkable features. I looked up at my parents and rolled my eyes and let out a sigh that was described to me later as "in the manner of a petulant thirteen-year-old girl who had just been told she could not attend some fucking stupid concert she had her little idiot heart set on." My folks were taken aback. Meredith posited that perhaps I had some sort of attitude problem. John offered that it might be best to nip this in the bud with some good old-fashioned corporal punishment. They called for the nurse.

"See? Look! There it goes," John said.

"Don't call it an 'it' dear; it's a he!" Meredith interjected.

"Barely," John muttered.

The nurse mused that perhaps it was indicative of some kind of palsy or retardation. "Whatever your baby is doing, it is pretty annoying," she said.

"What should we do?" John asked.

"Be patient. Consult with Dr. Chudley. Maybe it's just a temporary facial tic." I then turned my head and rolled my eyes and the nurse sighed. "I can only tell you that I understand that this must be very frustrating for you. It is inappropriate to want to hit a baby, but I feel it too," she said.

The more time they spent with me in the maternity ward, the more their hearts softened. My eye-rolling was frequent and irritating, but I had some redeeming qualities. I was, after all, a baby. And babies have this strange scent that naturally protects them from violence and ill will. It is the scent that can only be described as the very essence of humanity. My parents would take care of me to the best of their abilities. They both agreed that I was not likely to

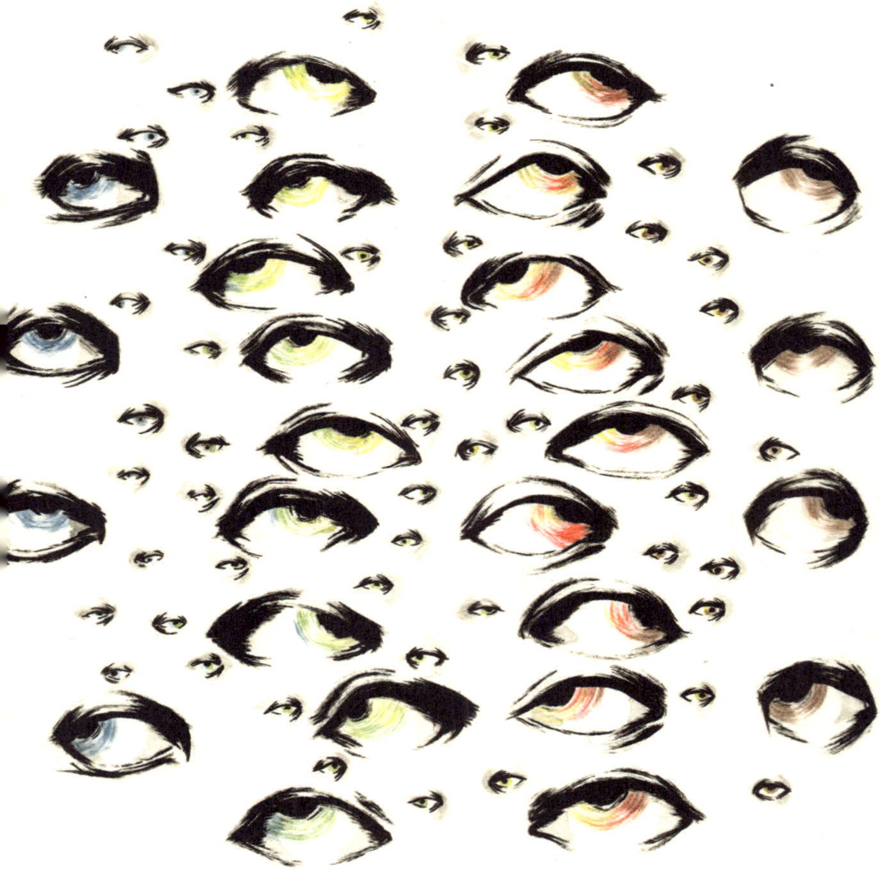

grow up to be much of a man, so they named me Leslie. When I was finally taken home, I was baptized by my sister, Frances, who spat in my face repeatedly.

When I was in elementary school and just beginning to learn the basic tenets of what it meant to be a socialized and literate human, my eye-rolling made relationships with teachers quite difficult.

It was Grade five. I sat in the principal's office after a particularly terrible flare up of my peculiar affliction.

"Leslie, if you don't stop rolling your eyes, I swear to Jesus, I will punch you in the face with my freaking fists. And I won't take off my rings!" Ms. Nichol said.

I rolled my eyes.

"I swear to Christ!"

"OK, calm down, Ms. Nichol," Mr. Duchamp, the principal, said. "Let's start from the top. Tell me about the incident."

"We were in the midst of a quiz about Confederation. And I asked the simplest of questions: 'What was the date of the Meech Lake Accord meetings?' Leslie said that he didn't know and then proceeded to roll his eyes at me. In front of the entire class. To show such disrespect to me is bad enough. But to roll your eyes at our national heritage? That is tantamount to treason, Mr. Duchamp!"

"Leslie, why do you hate Confederation so much?" Mr. Duchamp asked.

I rolled my eyes.

"What is your problem?" Ms. Nichol said.

"I don't want do it. It's a facial tic. I was born with it. It just happens when I get nervous. And I get really nervous a lot. I was born with it," I said.

Ms. Nichol closed the office door. Mr. Duchamp took out the strap. This was my favourite part.

PEN PALS

Constance Waterfield
115 Ash Street
Goose Creek, South Carolina
29445

Dearest Constance,

I procured your name and address from the personal advertisements of the most recent saddle-stitched issue of *Letters of Appreciation: The Official Newsletter of the Society for the Revival of Old-Timey Letter Writing in Contemporary Society*. How swiftly my blood flowed when I read your entry! "I must write to her post-haste!" I thought to myself. And now that very thought is in action. And ink is meeting paper! I do hope you will be my pen pal, my correspondence comrade as it were. (Note that I do not mean "comrade" in any communist sense of the word. I just enjoy the poetry of the phrase!) In an effort to persuade you, I shall now tell you à little bit about myself.

I am a forty-three-year-old teacher's assistant in Montreal — a backwater city of sorts — which is in Quebec, which is in Canada at the present, which is north of where you are in South Carolina. My work consists of hours of relative tedium — interacting with students, marking papers, and completing various tasks and doing so with a kindness and humbleness that was instilled in me from my earliest of days by my parents, Constance (that's your name, too!) and Jack Carberry. And almost beaten out of me by my dear, but particularly violent older sister, Gwendolyn. But, to this day, I assure you, I remain kind and humble. It's what sets me apart from other jerks. I often fear that assisting a teacher is not the most interesting of callings to most people but equally assured since you listed scholarship as one of your interests in your ad. Oh, the countless days I spend as an assistant to a pedagogue! Oh, the feats of administrative dexterity! I suppose if I were truly dexterous or computationally nimble, I would know the exact number of days, wouldn't I? Never the matter!

When you listed "watching over children" as another one of your interests, my heart leapt out of my chest and did a cartwheel. (Obviously, this didn't happen or I would surely be dead, but I felt it was a charming enough expression of my excitement, and upon my third edit of this letter, have decided to include it.) You see, one of the great joys of my life is my weekly visit to Laurier Park where I feed the pigeons (another shared hobby!) and watch the children play on and in their various play structures. Sometimes I fear for the more adventurous ones as they swing to and fro

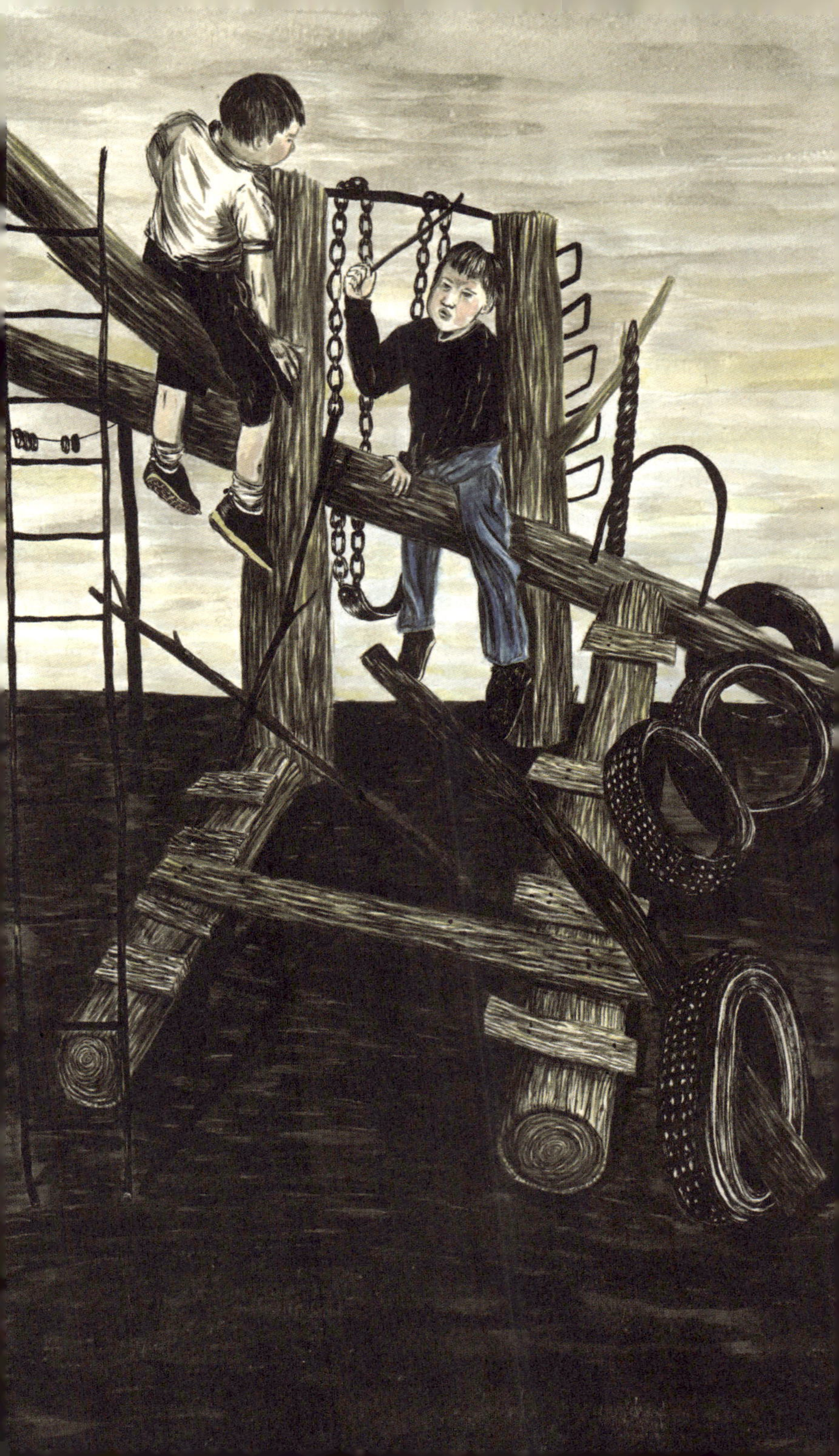

like our distant relatives, the monkeys, but you would be surprised at how few mishaps I have seen over the years. (Or perhaps you would not, since you have a children-watching habit of your very own!)

Oh, Constance, how the felicity multiplies! How many things we have in common! I wish I could will your response into my mailbox this very instant! I need your immediate response like oxygen!

Your new pen pal,
Winston Carberry

Winston Carberry
4650 Park Avenue
Montreal, QC
H2V 4E9

Dear Winston,

How nice to hear from one of our neighbors to the north. How is the socialist safety net treating you? I jest! I have never been to Montreal! Is it quite cold? It is warm here in South Carolina, and often hot even!

I am a tad concerned about something in your last (first!) letter. You claim that we have a similar hobby that is watching children. I wish to clarify that the children I watch over are my nieces and nephews. I am the designated babysitter for my family as I have no children of my own on account of my being incapable of getting pregnant. So, while I applaud your interest in the young people of your country, I am concerned that perhaps you may be doing something inappropriate by simply going to a park and watching random children play. Can you perhaps clarify what it is that you precisely mean and also what you aim to achieve by your children-watching activities? With the appropriate response, I can see no reason why we couldn't indeed become pen pals of a semi-regular variety and perhaps learn more about each other and indeed the human condition through our correspondence. Because isn't that always the way?

I await your clarification,
Constance Waterfield

Constance Waterfield
115 Ash Street
Goose Creek, South Carolina
29445

Dearest Constance,

I would like to take this opportunity, as I put pen to paper for the second time in the name of our correspondence, to clarify that, indeed, and without fail, I do not have any sexual predilection toward the youth of my nation, or any nation for that matter. I simply have a desire to keep children, particularly the shy, timid and weak ones from being hurt.

You see, as a child, I suffered from many beatings and tauntings. I have been told by many people that I am simply not very likeable. I remember countless recesses at school, where, in order to avoid eye contact and the resulting beatings, I would hide away. I had some interesting hiding places. My favourite hiding spot was underneath the large slide in the adjacent playground. There was a crawl space of sorts and I would huddle up there, hear the laughter and feel the weight of other children on my back as they came to the bottom. That brief anonymous contact made me feel like I was a part of things. It has been a difficult life in many ways. But I say this not for sympathy or to invoke a sense of pathos into this missive. I say this in order to bring you to the point of understanding why I watch the children in Laurier Park. I am a self-appointed civil servant of sorts! O, Constance, I constantly and vigilantly watch the children in order to protect the meekest of them from the most predatory!

When I visit the park, I make sure the children know, tacitly or explicitly, that they had better not engage in any form of bullying. I hope this clarification is the first step into the expansive world of ink-and-paper-bound camaraderie!

Eagerly,
Winston

PS: How long have you been barren?

Winston Carberry
4650 Park Avenue
Montreal, QC
H2V 4E9

Winston,

This is a difficult letter to write. I find that you write a very pleasing letter, aesthetically speaking. Your diction is quite unique. The content of your letters, however, is not as pleasing. Let me be clear. I don't think you should, in any way, engage children in any form of physical altercation. I am afraid I am going to have to terminate our Penpalship.

Constance

Constance Waterfield
115 Ash Street
Goose Creek, South Carolina
29445

My Dearest Constance,

I will miss you. Please reconsider. I am not a bad man.

Winston

Winston Carberry
4650 Park Avenue
Montreal, QC
H2V 4E9

Please cease and desist from any further communication.

Constance Waterfield

SYSTEMA VLAD

One block north of my house on St. Denis Street, there was a dojo, or training centre, or something, and it had a big red cursive neon sign that read: Systema Vlad. I had always been curious about the place. There were hardly ever any people exercising in there, but often late at night when I would return from a stroll, I would see a man, presumably Vlad, lying on top of someone, always a different woman, on a gym mat. Being the meek and shy sort, I decided to write a letter asking for more information about what exactly Systema Vlad was. A package arrived a week later with a DVD and a signed black and white 8 x 10 glossy of Vlad himself!

I popped in the DVD. The man on the television screen was an older Vlad than the one in the photo. He looked slightly out of shape, fairly hairy, but definitely formidable. He spoke in a very odd Russian accent. "Privyet! I'm Vlad from Systema Vlad! Thanks for watching my DVD, entitled

"Systema Vlad: How to Learn Systema From, Me, Vlad." In this video, I, Vlad, will discuss the topics of Systema: the Russian Martial Art of Fighting and Subduing People, Dissenters, or Bears. But first, watch this kick." He kicked into the air. "Ugh. Pretty cool right? You could kick like that too, if you study with me, Vlad. We will cover such topics as, Defending Yourself from Attacks from People, Dissenters or Bears, Attacking People, Dissenters or Bears, Throwing Large and Medium-Sized Shovels at Walls and Other Targets, Holding Someone Down on the Floor so They Can't Move whether They Are Friend or Enemy, and The Six Vital Parts of the Body to Attack that Will Hurt Most when Attacked! What are these six body parts you ask? Not so fast, droogy! That's Russian for "friends!" You can take a good guess but first you should come down to 5456 St. Denis in Montreal for live demonstration by me, Vlad, or one of my assistants, Guillaume or Stacy. Can you believe that Stacy is actually man? With name like Stacy? Well, he is! So, don't you worry! The cost is fifty dollars. That's not so many rubles, mofo! Now I will use my assistant, Guillaume, to show you more kicks and moves that will entertain you and make you want to study the system of Systema Vlad!"

Vlad seemed like a magician as he threw Guillaume about. I had to learn this magician's secrets. I vowed to myself that I would attend a free demonstration, and if it were as awesome as it looked, I would sign up.

His first words to me were: "Hold me!" So I held Vlad with an intensity that I had not been able to muster since my days of holding people. I had Vlad pinned to the ground, at my mercy. Or so I thought. Within seconds, Vlad had quickly shifted his weight and disturbed my balance. Then Vlad slipped out of my hands and reverse-pinned me, rubbing my face against the sticky blue gym mat.

"Yes! Very good!" exclaimed Vlad as he popped up onto his feet. "I have now shown you superior technique you can use on people weaker and less clever than me."

"That was very impressive."

"I am very impressive!"

"Yes, you are."

"I have just illustrated a famous Russian technique of being strong and fast!"

"What's it called?"

"Systema Vlad!"

"No. I mean the technique. What is that particular technique called?"

"It is called Systema Vlad! I am Vlad! You are Jesse, which is totally a girl's name like Stacy! It appears your entire culture is really into giving girls' names to men. No wonder it is so easy to be superior physically to you. I will be gentle, Jesse girl."

Vlad took me by the hand and dragged me over to an area of the gym where there was a wooden slab on the wall with various red and black dots. "Now is the time for the forceful throwing of shovels! Stacy will show you."

"I'm not entirely comfortable with shovels," I said.

"Don't be pussy. Hey, Stacy! Come here and meet another man fellow with a girl's name. This is Jesse. He desires to be strong like a tiger and not weak like fucking pussy!" A strapping, ponytailed, hairy man in tear-away track pants and a black muscle shirt swaggered over. His brow glistened with healthy sweat. I extended my hand and received a sideways high-five. Stacy then gestured that I make a fist, as he had done, and I complied. Stacy tapped my knuckles with a light-yet-firm amount of force.

"Fist bump, dude! Terrorist tap!" Stacy smiled.

"Very good," I said softly.

"OK, dude. Here's the deal. If you have the need to throw a shovel at some motherfucker, this is how you do it." Stacy gripped the handle of what looked like a gardening shovel with a sharpened tip. "You take the handle, and grip it like so. Tight. And then you isolate your target with your eyes. Your eyes are the key here. You throw with your eyes, not with your hand. Do you understand?"

"I think so."

"No. There is no 'think' about it, dude! Why would anyone 'think?' Bro, it's all about eyes and target acquisition and grip. Grip is important too."

"Well, you grip with your hand, right?"

"No. *Dude*. You grip with your *eyes*. Grip and rip! Got it?"

"Umm...got it."

"OK. Watch." Stacy flicked the shovel like a knife effortlessly and it landed smack dab in the middle of one of the many red dots on the slab. "*Dude*! Did you see that? Smack dab in the middle of a red dot! And not just any red dot. That was *the* red dot. That was my target, dude!"

"But you didn't identify that as your target, so there's no way I could really know that. I believe you and everything, but I'm just saying."

"Oh! Bro-dude! Bad move. Bad fucking move — questioning your master instructor of Systema."

"I didn't mean to offend."

"The only one you have offended is yourself."

"What?"

"Check it out dude. Up against the wall."

"What?"

"Get up against the wall. *Now!*" Stacy shoved me and then pinned me up against the giant wooden slab.

"Please don't."

Vlad peeked his head above Stacy's left shoulder. "Lesson you learn now is very important. Will you be pussy or tiger? Meow or Roar? Choice is yours unless you choose badly."

"Be cool. And you will step into the world of manhood," Stacy said.

"Hey, yes. Be extra super cool here as a favour to me, Vlad," Vlad said.

Stacy plucked the shovel out of the wall, took ten paces back, and held the shovel high in the air. "With the eyes!" he screamed.

I was drenched in sweat and trembling. "With the eyes," I whispered.

Stacy let the shovel fly and it tore right through my T-shirt sleeve. I felt nothing. And then I felt relief, until I saw the blood spurting out of my right arm. Vlad yelped. Stacy was laughing for some reason. I slumped to the ground.

"Wake up," Vlad said.

"We will be friends forever," I said with a heavy slur.

"Haha! Yes! The best! I will buy you slice of pizza!"

I can't remember much after that. I had been drugged and was sewn up. I remember looking down at my slice of pizza and thinking that it looked like the saddest slice of pizza in the world. I signed a waiver.

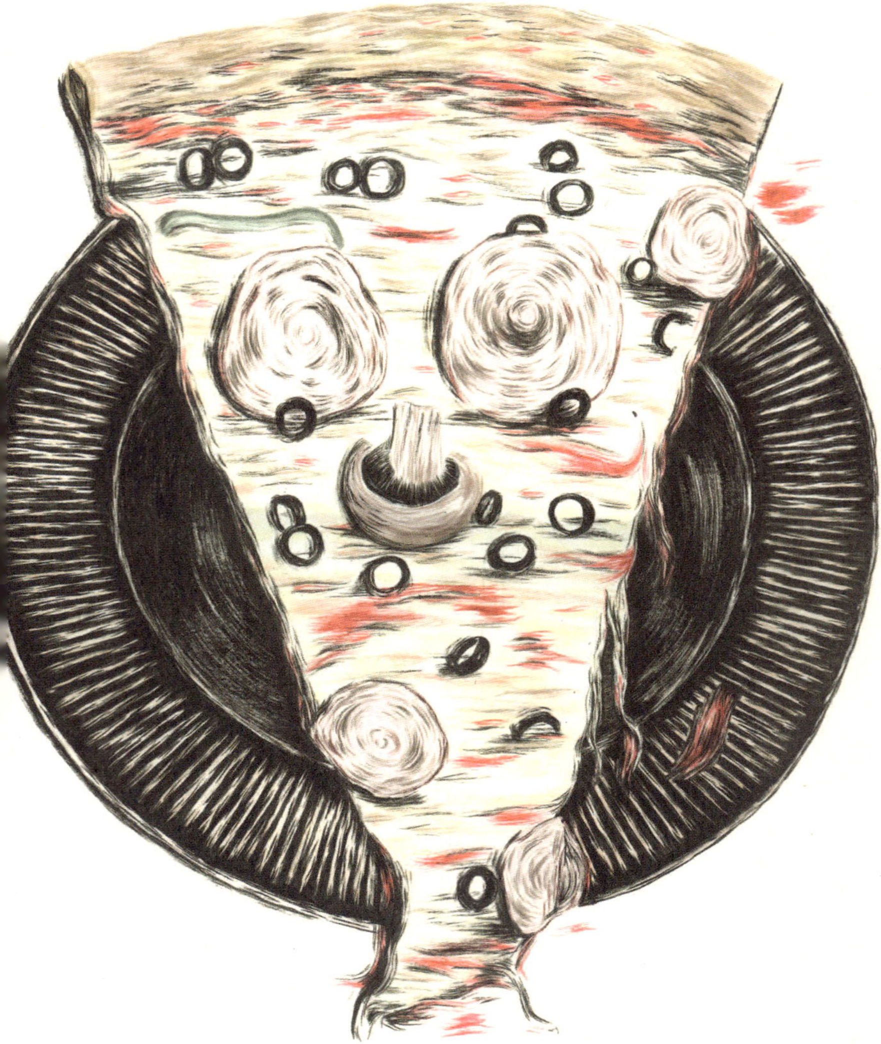

As the months rolled by, and I grew to appreciate Vlad and tolerate Stacy, and I became fairly proficient at the martial art of Systema. I figured I could toss or wrestle even the strongest of dissenters, maybe even a bear. Vlad took me out for ice cream and vodka on Sunday afternoons and we would often sit in an unpopular café on St. Laurent and play chess and discuss matters of Systema, world politics, and the heart.

"My advice you should take is this: have sex on top of many women! Let your seed plant inside of them and then they will be pregnant. Then go away as fast as you can! This way you will have your choice of many women and children to settle on!" Vlad said.

I advanced my bishop in order to threaten Vlad's rook, scooped a glob of strawberry sundae into my mouth and took a sip of Troika. "I don't think that's right for me, Vlad. I kind of don't even want sex so much. It's just belonging that I want. Belonging and security. You know, like just knowing someone is waiting at home for you, waiting for you to arrive with groceries and maybe then you will cook her a nice dinner and watch a movie or perhaps she will invite a friend over and have sex in front of you?"

"Jesse! This is not man's job! Cooking dinner!"

"Well, I like it."

"Gross. Well, listen my strange friend, you are one

weird fellow. Consider knocking up ladies. Stacy does it all the time! It makes him legend!"

"Doesn't he owe a lot of child support?"

"Not if he changes addresses lots he doesn't!"

"I don't know if that's responsible, Vlad. You know, I really care about the welfare of children."

"Ha! You are square! That's you!"

"Vlad?"

"Yes, my girlish friend?"

"Whatever happened to your other assistant? Guillaume?"

"Ah. Funny story. Guillaume doesn't exist anymore!"

"You mean...he's dead? What happened?"

"All I can tell you is it was funny story."

At Systema Vlad, I sparred with Stacy. My determination and confidence had improved exponentially. My moves were fluid as I lunged, ducked, and juked my way through my training. Stacy was impressed and slightly threatened. It felt like I was training him. I noticed Vlad slip in the back door and watch quietly as I pawed at and gripped Stacy. Vlad smiled. "Excellent mastery of Systema!" he yelled and slowly clapped. I foolishly looked over to Vlad and smiled. Stacy took advantage of the distraction and sucker-punched me in the gut. I clenched and dropped.

"But, Jesse, you can't distract yourself from menacing danger!"

I held my stomach and nodded. I looked up at Stacy and said "Time out." As soon as he nodded and turned, I tackled him and held his head against the mat, digging my unkempt nails into his neck. "If you ever sucker-punch me again, I will destroy you. Do you hear me?"

No response.

I applied more pressure, breaking the skin. "Do you hear me?"

"Fuck. Yes. God! Whatever!"

"Very awesomely executed! The key to all of Systema is to fight without honour! OK, fellows. Let's take five minutes!" Vlad said as he pulled me aside and handed me some stale water in a Gatorade bottle. "I need to be asking you one query, Jesse. Do you have driver's license, major credit card, and valid passport and also sense of adventure?"

"Well there are a lot of queries in that one query, but at this point I can honestly say yes to all of them."

"Very well then and good. We will go on an adventure. A road trip to Big Apple to find you woman! A soul maid!"

Within three days, the Prius was rented, the bags were packed and Vlad and I were on our first ever road trip. Brooklyn-bound. We made our way toward the American border. The snow was falling in slow, heavy flakes, *Days of Our Lives* style. And with around twenty minutes to go before entering Vermont, Vlad cranked up the Kenny Loggins and spoke the truest words ever spoken.

"In 1986, Kenny Loggins traveled back in time to Vienna, 1781. He consulted with Mozart. The result was 'Danger Zone.' OK, that probably didn't happen, but as you listen to this tune, it really feels like that is fucking fact! If I had to choose one defining characteristic of the Danger Zone Loggins is singing of, I would have to go with Danger. If you think about how many zones there are, it can be little overwhelming. But relax. There's only one Danger Zone. That's what matters, Jesse. And remember: almost every song ever written sucks precisely because it's not 'Danger Zone'."

"Wow, Vlad. That was beautiful!"

"Listen, Jesse," Vlad said in a strikingly domestic tone, "before we reach the border, I need you to know I'm not actually Russian. Not even close."

I sighed. "I know," I said.

"Really?"

"Yeah, well, the accent is very affected and inconsistent. Sometimes you sound Russian, other times you just sound confused. Also you never knew anything about Russia, its politics or its history, and so, you know, the whole thing was just obvious and offensive to everyone I think."

"Really? Seriously? Man. I thought I had that voice down pat. Because, you see, it's the key to my business. No one wants to learn the Russian art of Systema from a guy named Wenton Billingham."

"I am your only current client, Vlad, and I am not paying, so I think it may actually be hurting your business because of...Wait, what? Your name is Wenton Billingham?"

"Shut up, Jesse. You don't hear me making fun of your name."

"Yes, yes I do. All the time."

"But that is my *persona*."

"Well, I always thought if you dropped the unintentionally comedic and, frankly, hateful accent, then things might pick up for the business."

"Why didn't you ever say anything?

"I don't know, you are kind of my best friend, and I figured you needed to use that voice for some reason. Like self-esteem or something? I just wanted to be supportive."

"Jesus, Jesse. You are kind of my best friend too!"

"Do you mind if I still call you Vlad?"

"I would punch you in the fucking face if you didn't!"

I smiled and turned up the tunes. We were silent until we reached the border. I pulled up to the window and saw a thirty-something blonde border guard. She had mildly masculine features but was objectively attractive. Despite her furrowed brow, I had a sense that she probably had a big heart. I handed over the two passports.

"Destination?" the guard asked.

"Brooklyn, Ma'am," I responded.

"Brooklyn? What business do you have in Brooklyn?"

"None. That is to say, no business. Just pleasure. Well, maybe pleasure. If it works out. You could say that pleasure *is* our business!"

"I'm sorry? What is that supposed to mean?" The guard's tone grew colder and more impatient.

Vlad leaned over. "I got this Jesse," he said and looked up at the guard. "Ma'am, we are going down to Brooklyn in order to find a woman."

"What do you mean 'find a woman'?" she asked. "And sir, why are you crying?"

"Oh, well! My friend and I just — around fifteen minutes ago — we admitted to each other and declared to the world that we were best friends. It was a very emotional moment. And then we listened to some highly emotional tunage! Anyways, that's not the point. The point is, well, surely you've experienced love in your life?"

Silence.

"My friend here has to find a woman to fall in love

with and we are going to go follow her for a few days. A week, tops."

"Excuse me?"

"Oh. Well in a non-threatening way, of course. I feel that Jesse here needs to finally track down and nab a woman. I mean he is still a virgin. Which is very strange for a man his age, and I feel that this trip is mostly about letting loose and letting life happen, you know?"

I had to chime in — to clarify. "I've always tried too hard to control everything. I want to lose control, you know? I want to lose control in Brooklyn."

The guard stayed quiet for around thirty seconds as she typed in information from our passports. Then, gesturing, she said, "OK sir. Please pull the car over into one of those open spaces."

"Sure thing!" I said.

Twelve hours later, we were in Vermont and back on the road to Brooklyn. As the Lake Champlain region gave way to the Adirondacks, I became so jacked-up. There were all these beautiful trees. I didn't know what kind and neither did Vlad. But it would have been nice to know what kind of trees the nice trees were. If this were a third-person story then perhaps the narrator could tell you. But it's not. I put the highly irregular interrogation at the border in the back of my mind. I was so very eager to get to New York that I had increased my speed significantly. I did the calculations in my head and determined that there were five-and-a-half more hours to go. Five if I floored it. I inserted the best Tears for Fears CD, *The Hurting*, and belted out "Pale Shelter" as Vlad fell asleep.

Ten minutes passed and I glimpsed the red and blue flash of a State Trooper SUV behind us. I pulled to the side of the road, as my father had drunkenly taught me to do, and I put on my best face. The heavy-set, mustachioed trooper approached the Prius and gestured for me to roll down my window.

"Son, do you know how fast you were driving?"

"Good day to you, sir! I believe I was up to 140. I'm obviously in a hurry, so if we could make this quick…"

"Jesus Christ! Are you actually sassing me, boy? Don't sass me and don't insult my intelligence."

"Well that wasn't what…oh. I see. I'm sorry. I was using the metric system. It's what we use up in Canada. Marconi and all that. He invented the metric system. Smart man. Smart man, indeed. It's a shame you are still stuck in Imperial measurements. The metric! It's a far superior system. You see, if I were to answer your question again, using your antiquated system of measurement, I would say around eighty-six miles per hour, sir."

"Listen, dipshit, you were going eighty-seven miles per hour."

"So I was very close in my estimate!"

"Shut up! Let me tell you exactly what happens to guys like you. Do you want to hear what happens to guys like you?"

"Well, not really. As I said, I am in a hurry…"

"Holy goddamn shit! Shut the shit up! Guys like you. They speed. They speed and they listen to their hip-hop music about gangbanging and alternative lifestyles and they don't give a shitting shit about anyone or anything other than their own smug satisfaction and hedonism and ethnic music. And then guys like you take a sharp corner on the interstate, and then guys like you drive through the rail guard and die in a fiery twisted mess of metal, wretched humanity and … fire! And then guys like you get buried under a winter of heavy snow and the idiots who may love guys like you because they were unfortunate enough to give birth to you or share bunk beds with you or settle for you or some shitty shit like that have to wait until the spring for the chance to find the dead, mangled, unrecognizable bodies of guys like you!"

"With all due respect, I think that may be a mild mischaracterization…"

"Shut up. Just shut the shit up! Now sit here and think about how stupid you are for speeding while I write you up a ticket…a ticket for speeding."

The trooper handed me the ticket, and I drove away at sixty-five miles an hour. Vlad slept, murmuring in an almost-British upper-class accent. The Adirondacks gave way to the Catskills and the snow began to blow. It was eerily beautiful but equally daunting. I slipped in a Lionel Richie CD, specifically *Can't Slow Down,* and looked at the well-slept Vlad.

"Hey, my brother."

"Hey, Jesse."

"How do you feel, Vlad?"

"I feel like drinking. Have you ever had a best friend before?"

"No."

New York was hit with the worst snowstorm in years. And in the early evening Vlad and I pulled off the Brooklyn Bridge just in time for the aftermath. News jerks on the radio were calling it "Snowpocalypse," "Snowmageddon," "Snowmaclysm," "Snowtastrophe," and "Snowlocaust." For some reason beyond Vlad and me, the mayor of the city of New York decided not to plow the streets of Brooklyn. Cop cars, ambulances, taxis, and trucks were all stuck spinning their wheels, and it was very difficult for many people to get around, but Vlad and I just plowed on through on account of the winter tires on our Prius. Vlad had taken the wheel and drove with reckless abandon.

"Look at all of this!" Vlad said. He swerved around a stuck police car and onto the sidewalk, and continued to barrel down E. New York Avenue toward the Howard Johnson on Utica. "This would never happen in Montreal. In Montreal we know how to deal with a little bit of snow."

"But the news jerks are calling this a Snowmageddon," I said.

"Those news jerks are jerks. Think about it, Jesse. In Montreal, within an hour of the first flake, we have fleets of the world's finest snowplows cleaning it all up and making it safe for our citizens. And you know why?"

"Powerful unions? A well-planned city budget?"

"Well, maybe that's a part of it. But I would like to think that it's more to do with the Canadian heart. It is a superior heart to the American heart. Just think of all we've accomplished as a nation. No wars. No famine. No slavery. No problem!"

"I'm pretty sure we're at war right now with the Taliban in Afghanistan."

"Don't be naïve, Jesse."

There was the occasional Brooklynite on the street.

Some young men with shovels over their shoulders, some families trudging through the unplowed mess toward home. Vlad maneuvered the Prius the wrong way through a yield lane and onto Utica. The hotel was now in sight.

"This is amazing!" I said.

"We're kind of like action heroes right now!"

"We're *exactly* like action heroes right now!"

"We're like Mel Gibson and Danny Glover!"

"Yeah! Or like I'm Luke and you're Dak from *The Empire Strikes Back* and the Prius is our snowspeeder and the buildings are the AT-AT's!"

"Yeah! Totally! Except I'm driving, so I'm Luke and you're Dak, Luke's really excitable aerial gunner who dies almost immediately! You're him!"

"Right. But I don't want to die."

"Nobody wants to die, Jesse. Just take one for the team."

Vlad glimpsed a corner store and pulled to the side, put on the hazard lights, and went to get a twelve-pack of Budweiser. Vlad explained that it was important for him to drink twelve beers before sleep because if he didn't he would be shaking, sweating, and itching all night. And since we would be sharing a room, he thought it would be the right thing to do to spare me that experience.

Vlad walked swiftly around and through the Brooklyn

snowdrifts. A precious few snowplows lumbered down major streets and sidewalks. He looked back at me and smiled. He approached a large snow bank that was blocking his way across the street. He took a step back and leapt over the three foot bank. He leapt so gracefully, like the way one would lunge toward a person, dissenter, or bear. He didn't notice the snowplow that was barrelling along. The snowplow driver didn't notice Vlad. As he landed, he slipped. Then Vlad got plowed.

WHEN IT GOT
A LITTLE COLD

"Hey! That's St. Mary's Hospital! Do you know what you did there?"

"What, Daddy?"

"You got yourself born there! That's where I met my daughter!"

"Oh, yeah! St. Mary's Hospital. I remember!"

"What do you mean 'I remember?' You don't remember!"

"Sure, I do."

"Well, then tell me about it."

"You tell me first."

"OK. Well it was taking a long time and your mother was in a lot of pain. She had started to develop a fever. And her doctor told her that she had to have a c-section. Do you know what that is?"

"Yeah. That's when they cut open your belly to get the baby."

"Yeah. So your mom didn't want this, obviously. And you know how your mom is stubborn?"

"My mom isn't stubborn. She's just really smart."

"Well, whatever. She was insistent on not having a c-section so she started yelling at the doctor. I thought that was pretty cool because I never liked that old guy."

"Why didn't you like him? What did Mommy say?"

"I thought he was mean and cranky. I shouldn't say I didn't like him. I just liked other people more. Your mom said, 'Listen: you are going to go and get two buckets of ice and I will get my temperature down myself and I am going to have this baby the way I want to have this baby!'"

"Whoa! Did she really yell it like that?"

"Yeah. It was awesome. Your mom is very strong-willed."

"What does strong willed mean?"

"It's the same as stubborn, but a nicer way to say it."

"Oh. Strong-willed."

"Yeah. So the doctor stormed out of the room. And a new doctor came in. She was a really friendly French Canadian lady."

"What was her name?"

"I don't remember."

"You should remember her name, Daddy."

"I'm not good with stuff like that."

"But still. You should remember her name."

"The new doctor was super nice. And she came into the room with two buckets of ice. And sure enough, your mom managed to get her temperature down. It was pretty amazing to see. The new doctor told your mom that she was smart to suggest that. And then it was time for you to be born!"

"How did everyone know?"

"Well, your mom's vagina got really, really big."

"So I could fit through, right?"

"Exactly. And then, the strangest thing happened. The really nice doctor told me that she needed my help. She told me that you needed my help to get born. So she told me to…well…to put my hands where your head was and to apply pressure."

"Wait. Where was my head now?"

"You know…in your mother."

"In her vagina?"

"Yes."

"Oh, Daddy."

"Well, it's not like it was the first time I'd ever put my …I mean, this was different…I mean, you were there too. It's not…it's cool."

"It's cool?"

"Yeah."

"Well, I hope you washed your hands."

"So, I was like confused. I was pushing on your head, applying pressure like the doctor told me and I told the doctor that this seemed weird. Like, why was I pushing instead of pulling?"

"Daddy, this isn't the way Mommy tells the story."

"What do you mean?"

"Well, it's sorta the same but you're not really in it that much."

"That makes sense."

"That's OK?

"Yeah. Of course that's OK. It's called point of view. Your mom tells the story from her point of view. But listen, just as I was asking why I was pushing instead of pulling, you slid right out and right into my arms. It was the coolest thing ever. And you know what?"

"What?"

"You looked just like Gollum."

"Daddy!"

"Listen. What I'm going to tell you now is important. When I saw your face, it was so small and so compressed. And that compression was astonishing. It was as if everyone I loved was in your face. You looked like my mom and dad, your mom, my brother, my cousins, everyone. I saw you for the first time and I had this feeling that I had always known you and loved you. And I knew that I would always love you and protect you. You need to understand this. There are kids who never get to feel that they are loved. And you are so loved. Do you understand?"

"Yeah, Daddy. I understand. I love you too. It's cool. But now do you want to hear my story of it from my point of view?"

"OK."

"So, OK. It was very late at night."

"Early evening."

"Right. It was early evening. And I was just sort of figuring out how I was supposed to get out of my mom. And I was swimming around and looking for some light. And then it got a little warm and then it got a little cold. And when it got a little cold, I saw this light and felt this hand on my head. And the next thing I knew, I was in this guy's arms. I thought that this guy looks very much like a daddy. And there were all these other people there dressed up in weird blue outfits. And I said, 'Wah! Wah! Wahhhh!' and I thought, What is all of this? Who are you people? Why am I covered in blood? Are you people some sort of vampires? Why are you cutting my umbilical cord? That's how I eat! What is this, even? This is so not cool! And then you know what?"

"What?"

"I got to meet Mommy and that was pretty cool."

TEEN WOLF QUOTES
SLAVOJ ŽIŽEK

When do I actually encounter the Other 'beyond the wall of language', in the Real of his or her being? Not when I am able to describe her, not even when I learn her values, dreams, and so on, but only when I encounter the Other in her moment of jouissance.

Love feels like a great misfortune, a monstrous parasite, a permanent state of emergency that ruins all small pleasures.

We feel free because we lack the very language to articulate our unfreedom.

MR. SPOCK SAYS THINGS FROM EPISODES OF *GIRLS*

SORRY I PASSED YOU AN STD BUT I REALLY ENJOY YOUR QUIRKY WEB PRESENCE

I GUESS IT'S CLASSIC TO HAVE TO MASTURBATE 8-16 TIMES A NIGHT UNTIL YOUR LEGS SHAKE AND YOU'RE CRYING AND YOU'RE TRYING TO MAKE SURE YOUR PARENTS DIDN'T HEAR YOU SO YOU CHECK THEIR DOOR 8 TIMES

I WANT YOU TO KNOW, THE FIRST TIME I FUCK YOU, I MIGHT SCARE YOU A LITTLE, BECAUSE I'M A MAN AND I KNOW HOW TO DO THINGS

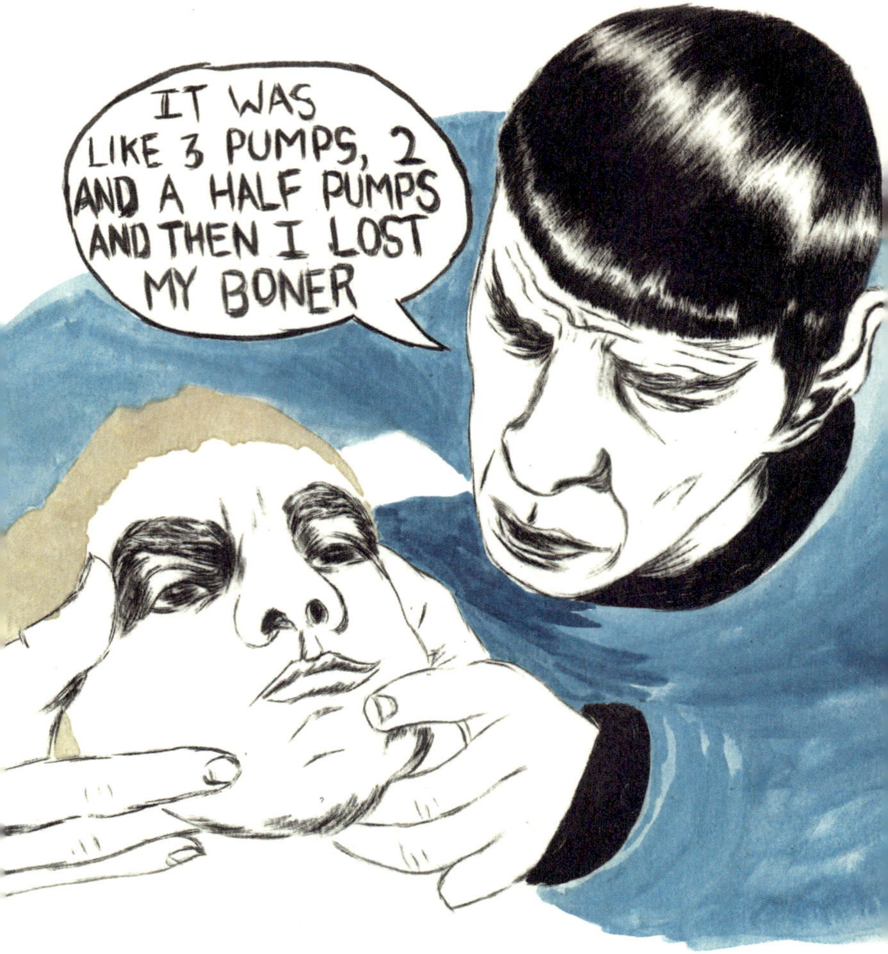
IT WAS LIKE 3 PUMPS, 2 AND A HALF PUMPS AND THEN I LOST MY BONER

JON PAUL FIORENTINO INTERVIEWS HIS MOTHER

JPF: Well, Mom, I'm 38 now. In what ways do you think I can do better?

MOM: Let me count the ways (laughter). I noticed you seem to have your days and nights mixed up and you don't manage money well. You have trouble paying parking tickets and bills on time. I think you need to be proactive instead of reactive. I wish you had more money so you could afford a personal assistant. Also: stop getting parking tickets.

JPF: You and Dad lived a fairly typical suburban life. You were educators and still are community leaders. Does it bother you that your weirdo sons both dedicated their lives to the arts and live in relative squalor?

MOM: No. We're happy that you boys are pursuing your

dreams and sharing your talents. Living in "squalor" is your choice. We didn't raise you in "squalor." I think we spoiled you too much.

JPF: I remember getting away with a lot of things as a teenager. Was I actually getting away with things or did you secretly know what I was up to?

MOM: I knew everything you were up to. At least I think so. I knew because I was the guidance counsellor to your best friends. I knew their habits and assumed they were yours. I found suspicious twigs in the drawer in your bedroom.

JPF: You spied on me?

MOM: No. I found the evidence after you moved out.

JPF: So you never spied on me?

MOM: No. Never.

JPF: Well, pot was just the tip of the iceberg. That's typical kid stuff.

MOM: Oh, I know.

JPF: You were my ninth grade Sex-Ed teacher. This was a particularly difficult experience for me and I imagine for you also. How was I as a student? I seem to recall not being particularly focused.

MOM: You were a pudgy, pubescent pain in the butt. You sat in the front and raised your hand wildly like Horshack from *Welcome Back, Kotter* and tried to answer every question: "Mom! I know! I know!" Also, your notebooks were in total disarray. You lacked focus.

JPF: I don't remember that. I remember being mortified and wanting it to end.

MOM: Oh, yes. The hardest part for me was trying to ignore you. You wanted to show everyone that you knew everything about the subject. (Laughter.)

JPF: What? Wow. I guess I blocked that out. For the most part I was so shy in high school. There was one English teacher (I won't name names) who didn't think I was particularly bright or creative. I was daydreaming all the time and he was kind of mean to me. Do you remember him?

MOM: I know exactly who you are talking about. His inability to encourage you and see your talent was a symptom of his own lack of knowledge and sensitivity. What would he say now about your success, I wonder.

JPF: Some of my books deal with weird and very "adult" things. Does this annoy you?

MOM: Yes. Lots of your writing can be funny or poignant. But I cannot read some parts because we are spiritually quite different. And I have a different morality. I suppose that's one other way you can do better.

JPF: One of the reasons I consider you and Dad to be my heroes is that you were always looking out for the outsiders and making sure they felt less alone. I still remember that all the teenagers in Transcona used to call you "Mom." So thank you for setting that example for me. I love you.

MOM: Thanks, Jonny. Love you too!

ACKNOWLEDGEMENTS

"I'm Not Scared of You or Anything" appeared in *Broken Pencil*.

"The Parable of Bryan Dong" appeared in *Joyland*.

"When It Got a Little Cold" appeared in *The National Post*.

"Jon Paul Fiorentino Interviews His Mother" appeared in *The National Post*.

Thanks to Mike Spry, Ian Orti, Darren Bifford, David McGimpsey, Jessica Rose Marcotte, Tyler Morency, Marisa Grizenko, Adam Seward, Heather O'Neill, Jennifer Lambert, Mark Medley, Hal Niedzviecki, Tara Flanagan, Shazia Hafiz Ramji, Karen Green, and my parents.

Special thanks to Maryanna Hardy and Brian Kaufman.

Very special thanks to Lilly Fiorentino.

This book is dedicated to The Thread.